DIVINE DOMINATION

Bought by the Billionaire
Book Four

By Lili Valente

DIVINE DOMINATION

Bought by the Billionaire
Book Four

By Lili Valente

Table of Contents

About the Book

WARNING: It's Book Four. You know what you're in for by now—more heat, more suspense, more head games, and more Jackson f*cking Hawke.

When Jackson gets his hands on the men who kidnapped Hannah, he's going to rip their hearts, still beating, from their chests.

Or worse.

No amount of pain or desecration seems sufficient punishment for the sin of taking Hannah away from him.

He won't stop until he has the woman he loves back in his arms and in his bed. But as the ugly truth behind his and Hannah's intertwined pasts is revealed, their love will face its greatest challenge yet.

* * Divine Domination is the 4th and final installment in the Bought by the Billionaire romance series. For maximum enjoyment it should be read after books 1, 2, and 3.* *

Author's Note

The Bought by the Billionaire series is a dark romance with themes that may be disturbing to some readers. Read at your own risk.

Dedicated to the dreamers

Also by Lili Valente

The complete Under His Command Series
Available Now:

Controlling Her Pleasure (Book One)

Commanding Her Trust (Book Two)

Claiming Her Heart (Book Three)

The Bought By the Billionaire Series
Available Now:

Dark Domination (Book One)

Deep Domination (Book Two)

Desperate Domination (Book Three)

Divine Domination (Book Four)

Learn more at www.lilivalente.com

CHAPTER ONE

Ian Hawke

The kid didn't stand a chance.

That's what people said about Ian when he was a little boy, growing up in the projects of inner-city Chicago, hiding under the bed while his mother turned tricks to keep the heat turned on and a needle in her arm.

That's what they said when he came to

school wearing the same dirty sweater for months. When the lice infestations got so bad the school nurse was forced to shave his head. When he grew more and more withdrawn until most of his classmates couldn't remember his name.

But what no one realized was that Ian was different than the other lost and forgotten children. He was special, the one in a million person who could live without love or kindness and who bounced back stronger every time the world knocked him down.

Later on in his life, the words "sociopath" and "psychopathic tendencies" would be bandied about by social workers and one of his more astute commanding officers, but Ian only accepted one label—survivor. He was a survivor and he was going to come out on top or die trying.

When he was still too young to go to school, Ian lay on the filthy floor beneath his mother's bed while she entertained her clients. He studied the delicate legs of the dead bugs littering the ground beneath the ancient four-poster, tuning out the sound of the squeaking mattress as he imagined the house he'd have when he grew up. It would be a mansion with a hundred rooms and a flock of servants to clean them. And if he discovered dust under a bed or a dead bug curled in a corner, he would punish the housekeeper responsible until she understood that Ian required excellence from everyone and everything associated with Hawke Manor.

His mansion would be like Wayne Manor, Batman's house, but even bigger, without any stuffy butlers bossing him around or bat caves hidden beneath it.

Ian didn't want to save humanity or even Gotham City. He just wanted to be bigger, meaner, and richer than anyone else and he wanted the entire world to know it. Once he was grown and richer than Batman, no one would look at him with pity in their eyes. They would look at him with respect or fear or they wouldn't look at him at all.

He didn't mind being invisible. There were times when he preferred to fade into the background, becoming part of the shadows until the moment he chose to make his presence known. It was an art he'd mastered before he learned to walk, a necessary survival technique growing up in a home with a short-tempered mother and an endless stream of johns who were never happy to see a kid hanging around.

By age three, Ian was a master of camouflage. By age six, he'd learned to use his ability to blend in with a crowd to hunt for the things he needed. At first he hunted food—stealing from the local bodegas and then the fancy grocery stores downtown, acquiring a taste for the finer things he wouldn't have known existed without his swift, clever hands.

As he grew older, his criminal proclivities expanded. He learned to hunt for wallets and expensive clothes and pretty girls, the kind who wouldn't give him the time of day if they knew where he'd come from and all the terrible things he'd done. He hunted drugs to sell, weapons to defend himself, and enough money to escape the neighborhood and make his dreams come true.

But then, days after his eighteenth birthday,

Uncle Sam stepped in and changed the course of his life, drafting him into his first tour of duty in Vietnam. Uncle Sam put an even bigger, better gun in Ian's hand, money in his pocket, and, most wonderful of all, gave him free rein to kill.

And kill he did.

Ian slaughtered the enemy with impunity and was happier in the dark, bloody jungle than he had ever been before. He was finally at home, in a place where monsters like him could run free. He loved war the way some men loved women or booze and by the time Stewart Mason was drafted into his platoon, Ian had served two tours of duty and advanced to the rank of Sergeant of his own squadron.

Mason was the softest of the new recruits, the son of a billionaire. He'd never held a gun before basic, let alone had to defend himself against the horrors of the world. His daddy's money had always done that for him.

The other higher-ups gave the kid two months, tops, but Ian saw something in Mason. The boy was soft and inexperienced, true, but behind his pale blue eyes lurked a devil waiting to be born.

In the humid jungles of Vietnam, Ian helped to birth Mason's darkness, awakening a blood lust in the other man that confirmed they were similar creatures. He taught Mason to hide, to hunt, and to kill with a ruthless efficiency that left entire villages decimated in the blink of an eye.

For the first time in his life, Ian had a true friend, a brother-in-arms and a brother of the soul. Mason understood what it was like to look out at the world and realize there was nothing to be afraid of. They were the predators, the top of the food chain, the masters of their blood-soaked kingdom.

But nothing beautiful lasts forever.

Children grow, love dies, and wars end.

Mason was pulled out in 1973, near the official end of the war. Ian followed two years later, escaping in one of the last helicopters during the fall of Saigon. He'd served six tours of duty without serious injury, but as the helicopter lurched into the sky he took two bullets in the leg, the shots fired by someone in the mass of South Vietnamese crowding around the embassy, desperate to be evacuated before the North took over.

He was recuperating in a military hospital in D.C., mourning the loss of the life he'd known and wondering if he would ever find a place as perfect as his terrible, wonderful jungle, when Stewart Mason walked into his hospital room.

Mason's father was dying and soon the family's estate would pass to the next generation. Stewart had three older brothers—Aaron, Ezra, and Matthew—as well as a much younger sister, Sybil. Each of the boys was slated to inherit one-fourth of their father's fortune while Sybil would inherit the summer house on the lake and a smaller trust fund.

"She isn't Dad's." Stewart's lips curved in a wry smile as he re-crossed his legs for the fifth time. He seemed to find the hard wooden chair beside Ian's bed as uncomfortable as his lone other visitor, the hospital psychologist. "But she's never been well and he's too soft to cut her out of the will."

Ian grunted. "I would have cut her out the moment I knew she wasn't mine. Right after I kicked her mother out of the house without a penny."

"No, you wouldn't." Stewart laughed. "You've got too much pride. You would have found another way to deal with the problem." His smile faded and a new tension crept into his voice, signaling that they were getting down to business. "And that's why I'm here. I have a proposition for you."

Ian searched Mason's face, not surprised to see the devil dancing behind his friend's eyes. "I'm listening."

"You know my brothers hate me," Mason said, keeping his voice low so as not to be overhead by the patients on either side of Ian's tiny partition. "If they inherit three-fourths of the estate, they'll stick together and shut me out. They'll ignore my advice and squander everything Dad fought so hard to build. If I don't do something now, in fifty years there won't be anything left. I've seen it happen before. No one is too rich to lose it all, not even us."

"So you want to find a way to have them written out of the will?" Ian feigned ignorance, resisting the urge to smile when Mason shot him an incredulous look.

"No, I don't want them written out of the will," he said in a harsh whisper. "I want them out of the picture. Permanently. And I want you to be the one to do it."

"Why me?" Ian asked, keeping his expression neutral. "Why not keep it in the family? We both know you're capable."

"I'll also be the first person the authorities will suspect. My alibi has to be airtight. While you're getting the job done, I'll be attending parties in the city, skiing upstate, and making sure I'm never near my brothers and never alone."

"But if I'm caught, it could still lead back to you," Ian said, his mind already clicking through possible assassination methods. "I wouldn't say who hired me, but we served together. There are records."

"You won't be caught. That's why I'm here. Because you're the best." Warmth softened Stewart's usually cool blue eyes. "You're my real brother. And if you help me, I'll make sure you never want for anything for the rest of your life."

Ian studied his friend, his brother, a part of him wanting to take the job with no more questions asked. But he knew Mason as well as he knew himself and realized the other man didn't appreciate anything that came too easily.

"I'll think about it." He relaxed back onto the too-thin pillows propped beneath his shoulders. "Come see me next week and bring your best offer."

"I'll give you my best offer now," Mason said, leaning closer. "I said you're my brother and I meant it. Do this for me and you'll have fifty percent."

Even Ian, a master at controlling his emotions, couldn't hide his surprise. "Half. Of everything?"

"Half of everything," Mason confirmed. "Half of three billion is a lot more than the twenty-five percent I'll be getting if my brothers inherit. I'll still be coming out on top, and I'll have a partner who understands that sometimes we have to make hard choices to make the most of our lives."

Ian concentrated on his breathing, drawing in long slow breaths and letting them out to the count of five. It was everything he'd ever wanted, handed to him on a silver platter, but he couldn't start counting the money or building his mansion yet.

He had to stay calm, stay smart, and make sure this went off without a hitch.

"I'll need time to heal," he said. "I can't start something like this with a bum leg. And I'll need information on all the targets. Everything you can get me."

"I'm already working on that." Mason cast a glance over his shoulder as one of the floor nurses bustled by with a tray of water glasses. "We have some time. Dad should have a few months left, maybe more. The disease is progressing rapidly, but he has the best doctors money can buy."

The best that money can buy.

Ian had never had the best that money could buy. He'd had the best that he could steal, snatching riches away from the people who hoarded them and running like hell before they could snatch them back. He couldn't imagine what it would be like to know he had all the money he would ever need, all the power he'd ever dreamt of.

And all he had to do was snuff out a few lights.

He'd already snuffed out hundreds, maybe thousands. He'd lost track of his tally by this third tour of duty, but he was undoubtedly an efficient killing machine unimpeded by remorse or regret. There wasn't a man or woman alive who was truly innocent. Innocence was for very small children and even they were simply seeds waiting to open, holding their potential for evil tight inside of them until it grew large enough to burst free.

Ian didn't believe in the sanctity of life. He believed in his own survival and his right to do as he pleased. He spared no one and he trusted no one…not even his best and only friend.

"All right," he said after a long moment. "But I'll need half of the money up front."

Mason's eyes flicked to the right, gazing over Ian's shoulder through the filmy window that overlooked the parking lot below. "I can't do half, but I can have an untraceable, fully laundered two million in the account of your choice by tomorrow morning. The rest will have to wait until I inherit. I won't have access to that kind of capital until then."

Ian cocked his head. "Most people look to the left when they're lying."

"I'm not lying." Mason shifted his gaze back to Ian, his face an expressionless mask. "And I won't be back next week. Take the deal now, or I'll find someone else. I'd rather be partners in this, but I don't have time to waste. I'm not going to let everything I deserve slip through my fingers because you aren't sure you can trust me."

And why should I trust you? Ian thought.

Mason was planning to have his family members murdered so that he wouldn't have to learn how to share. No matter how much Ian admired Mason's predatory instincts or how many times they'd saved each other's skins in combat, he would be a fool to jump into this without some serious thought.

Mason was dangerous. But he also wasn't the kind to make idle threats. If he said this was Ian's one shot, it was his one shot, and he wasn't about to piss away his chance to have everything he'd ever wanted.

"I'll call you with the bank account information this afternoon," Ian said, not missing the way Mason's shoulders relaxed away from his ears at the news.

Maybe his friend was sincere about wanting a partner. Or maybe he was simply relieved not to have to seek out another monster to get the job done. Truly excellent monsters— the kind who are crazy enough not to care about society's rules, but sane enough to cover their tracks—are few and far between.

Mason rose from his chair, reaching out to clasp Ian's hand tight. "Thank you, brother. You won't regret this."

Ian nodded. "And neither will you, as long as you keep your word."

Mason smiled, a hard curve of his mouth. "I'm ambitious, but I'm not a fool. You'll get everything you've been promised and more."

"I don't need more," Ian said. "Half is enough."

And it would have been. One point five billion dollars would have made his wildest dreams come true.

But on the cold December morning when Mason was named the sole heir to his father's vast fortune, the money never came. Ian's bank balance remained steady—not a penny more, not a penny less.

At three o'clock, he called Mason, but there was no answer, only a busy signal that droned in his ear, summoning the rage bubbling inside of him closer to the surface. At five o'clock, he drove by the row house in the elite part of D.C. where Mason had lived since he began his work as a lobbyist, but the house was empty. A glance in the windows revealed that the furniture was gone and the floors bare.

Even before Ian returned home to find an envelope slipped beneath his door, he knew he'd been cheated.

The message the missive conveyed

confirmed it—

If you talk, you'll go to jail, and you'll go alone.

There is no paper trail, no money trail, nothing to prove you weren't acting on your own. This is your chance to walk away. Take what you've been given, make a life for yourself, and don't attempt to contact me again.

If you do, you die. I've hired security and they've been instructed to shoot on sight.

Goodbye and good luck.

The note was typed with no signature, nothing to point to Mason. Ian wasn't surprised. Mason was as careful as he was greedy and had enough money to hire a small army to protect him. If Ian tried to take his revenge now, it would be a suicide mission. It would take time for his former friend to drop his guard, time that would be best put to use in planning and preparation.

Ian was a patient man. He was also a determined one.

He might have lost the battle, but he would win the war. By the time he was finished with Stewart, cheating a Hawke would be his greatest regret.

And now, just days from his sixty-fifth birthday, his moment had finally arrived. He'd failed once before, but now he had his hands on the only things Stewart truly cared about.

He had one of Mason's daughters locked away in a remote location in the Florida Keys and he had the other on his private plane looking up at him with frightened blue eyes the exact shade as her father's.

"As for what I want...." Ian settled onto the small leather couch next to Hannah Mason's seat, close enough to smell the grass and perfume scent drifting from her body. "I want your father to pay his debt. If he does, you will be allowed to live."

Hannah swallowed and her taut features relaxed, making it obvious she had no clue that he was talking about so much more than money.

No amount of money could right Mason's wrongs. There was only one way to even the score. Mason would pay his debt with the blood of his children, the keepers of his legacy.

What good was an empire, after all, without someone to pass it on to? Money could be replaced; not so little girls.

And Hannah and Harley were the last living Masons of their generation. Ian had already taken care of their cousins, those tragically unlucky men and women he'd orphaned when they were so very young.

"I think he'll choose you, anyway." Ian smiled at the pretty thing peering up at him, not surprised his son was smitten with her.

Hannah was beautiful, with a sweet heart that shone in her eyes and a brightness of soul found only in the very young and very breakable. She was one of the fragile, gullible, victims of the world fools like Jackson couldn't resist taking under their wing. He had assumed Jackson had learned the dangers of caring too much after the other sister had ruined his life, but apparently his son was a glutton for punishment.

"You're the good girl, aren't you?" Ian continued, knowing that she was. He knew everything about her, from the hobbies she'd enjoyed as a child to her grade point average when she graduated from college. "The one who always did as she was told? I understand your sister was his favorite once, but when he realizes he can only keep one daughter, I suspect he'll see the wisdom in sparing your life instead of hers."

Ian paused, watching the color drain from Hannah's face and her hands begin to shake. She seemed to be getting the message loud and clear, a fact she confirmed when she bent double and was sick all over the floor.

He watched, taking pleasure from her pain, determined to relish every moment of his hard-won, long-awaited revenge.

CHAPTER TWO

Jackson

Jackson had killed before—in combat and once when negotiations with a Mexican drug cartel had gone awry and he'd had no choice but to kill or be killed—but he had never experienced anything like the blood lust pulsing through his veins as he steered the abandoned golf cart he'd found at the airstrip back toward the villa.

When he got his hands on the men who had kidnapped Hannah, he was going to rip their hearts, still beating, from their chests and stuff the organs down their throats. He was going to pull them limb from limb and toss the pieces of their mutilated bodies into the sea. Or maybe he'd leave them out for buzzards to pick at and maggots to writhe inside.

Every fate he imagined for the men was more horrible than the last, but no amount of terror, pain, or desecration seemed sufficient punishment for the sin of taking Hannah away from him.

And if Dominic were correct, and the men intended to kill her…

Jackson swallowed hard, forcing down the gorge rising in his throat.

They would beg for death by the time he was through with them. They would *beg* for it. Jackson had no doubt he could deliver enough suffering to make Hannah's kidnappers sorry they'd ever heard her name, but that wouldn't bring her back. Once she was gone, she would be gone forever—and his heart and soul along with her.

He had to get to her before it was too late for both of them.

He parked the cart by the lanai and took the steps up to the villa two at a time. He found Eva and Dominic in the kitchen talking animatedly in Spanish, but their conversation cut off abruptly when he entered the room.

"I was too late." Jackson aimed himself at the phone, where Hannah had called her aunt nearly every day for the past month, trying not to think about the way her sweet laughter had filled the room as she chatted with the woman who was like a mother to her.

He would hear that laughter again. But first he would hear the screams of the men who had taken her away from him.

"They left on a small private plane," he continued. "The jet is still here, but I can't fly it. I'll have to hire a charter and see how fast they can—"

"We can take my jet," Dominic said. "I've already put in a call to the pilot in Moorea. He should be landing soon. And I've got a tech team hacking into a surveillance satellite orbiting the area. Hopefully, they'll be able to get a visual and tell us where the plane is headed."

Jackson slammed the phone back into the receiver before turning to shoot Dom his most threatening look. "Who are you? Who are you working for and why should I trust you when you knew Hannah was in danger and failed to protect her?"

"I'm working for her father, Stewart Mason," Dom said, as his mother angled her body in front of his, clearly intending to protect her son from Jackson, even if her employer was twice her size. "I've been working for Mr. Mason for years, trying to keep Hannah safe from those who mean her harm."

Dominic paused, eyes narrowing as he shook his head back and forth. "And then you showed up. At first, I thought you were part of it. But you really have no idea, do you?"

"No idea about what?" Jackson growled.

"About your father," Dom hurried on, clearly sensing Jackson's mounting frustration. "He's the one who killed Hannah's cousins.

He's trying to take out all of Stewart Mason's heirs."

Jackson's brows drew together so sharply it sent a flash of pain through his temples. "My father is a real estate developer. He's a cold hearted bastard, but he doesn't kill people." He frowned harder. "And even if he did, why would he give a shit about Mason's money or his heirs? My father is a wealthy man. The last thing he needs is more money."

"Story too long," Eva piped up, waving a hand at Jackson before turning back to her son. "Is too long and Hannah in trouble. You work together. Help her. Then you fight."

The seemingly sincere concern in the older woman's voice reminded Jackson of his other source of information, the one person he trusted wanted nothing but the best for Hannah. "I'm calling her aunt." He snatched the phone up with one hand as he pointed at Dom with the other. "Get my cell from the floor in Hannah's room. As soon as I'm finished with this call, I have to place another one. Then we'll talk."

He should probably call the Titan group

first. He doubted Alexander Titan would initiate an execution based on a text message—especially since they'd never discussed the price for murder on demand—but Hannah was his first concern.

He would do what he could to keep Harley safe, but only after he found out who had Hannah and was on his way to getting her back.

Sybil answered on the third ring, saying, "Hello, darling, is everything all right?" in a sleepy voice.

A glance at the clock above the stove revealed it was nearly midnight. Jackson had been so terrified he hadn't even noticed the time.

"No, Sybil, it's not. This is Jackson, Hannah's friend," he said, wincing at the last word. He was so much more than her friend, but her aunt had never met him or seen him and Hannah together. She might not trust him enough to open up about their family secrets, but he had to try, for Hannah's sake. "I'm sorry to be the one to tell you this, but something terrible has happened. Hannah's been taken. By two men, one of whom I thought I could trust with my life."

"Oh my God," Sybil whispered.

"I realized she was missing and followed them, but it was too late," he continued, knowing he didn't have time to waste explaining all the finer—and crazier—details of Hannah's abduction. "I got to the airfield in time to see their plane take off. My plane is still here, but I don't have a pilot so I couldn't follow them."

"Hannah's been taken," Sybil said, speaking to someone on the other end of the line. "And her friend can't fly the plane. Do you think—"

"There's a man here who claims he works for Hannah's father," Jackson broke in. "He says there's a plane on the way that we can use to go after her, but I don't know if I can trust him."

"Well, you don't really have a choice, do you?" Sybil's voice was surprisingly strong and steady. "You have to get to her as soon as possible, Jackson. If they took her alive, she won't be alive for long. I've already lost three brothers and four nieces and nephews to this nightmare. I can't lose Hannah, too. She's like a daughter to me."

Jackson leaned against the kitchen counter, fear prickling across his skin. Could Dominic be right about his father?

"The man here said that someone is killing the Mason heirs," he said, deliberately keeping things vague to see if Sybil would confirm Dom's claim. "Do you know why? It might help me figure out where they've taken Hannah."

"It has something to do with my brother, Stewart," Sybil said after only a moment's hesitation, evidently deciding to trust him. "Over the years, he's received threats from an old business partner. But when I've pushed for more information about the threats or the partner, he refuses to speak about it or to go to the authorities for help. He has deliberately kept the assassinations of our family members a secret while concealing the other man's identity and I... Well, I believe I know why."

"Why?" Jackson pressed, his thoughts racing.

Was his father the old business partner? It was easy to imagine Ian bending the law to crush a rival, but murder wasn't part of the tax code. As far as Jackson knew, his father had never even had a parking ticket. He was a decorated Marine, a self-made man who had married into one of the oldest families on the eastern seaboard. He wasn't a mob boss for God's sake.

You were a decorated Marine, and look how far you've fallen.

Maybe you inherited more from dear old dad than height and the color of your eyes.

"I think Stewart had something to do with what happened to our brothers," Sybil said in a pained voice. "He's always been different and they bullied him terribly when he was small. I was the only one who was kind to Stewart and I am the only one who didn't meet with an unfortunate accident in the fall of 1975, just weeks before our father's will was set to be read."

She sighed, the sound making it clear how heavily her suspicions had weighed on her. "I've had too much time to think to believe that's a coincidence. I was spared because Stewart told the person he'd hired to kill the others to let me live. But then, I assume something must have happened to make the killer turn on him." She paused before continuing in a haunted tone, "And now Stewart has spent the past forty years defending his family from a nightmare that he set in motion, knowing his connection to the murderer would be obvious if anyone ever learned the man's name."

"You could be right," Jackson said, his throat tight. "I'm going to look into a few things, Sybil. I'll call you back."

"I'll come to you," Sybil said. "My friend Hiro is a pilot. He says he can borrow a plane and get us both there in ninety minutes. When you figure out where they've taken Hannah, we'll come with you."

Her friend, Hiro. Jackson was tempted to tell the woman her trust was grossly misplaced but resisted the urge.

Hiro had been his spy, but he'd also said he cared about Sybil and sounded like he meant it. If there was one thing Jackson had learned from his time on the island, it was that people could change. Even the hardest heart could soften in the hands of the right person. Hannah had transformed him, given him back his soul and a reason for living. If Sybil had done the same for Hiro, Jackson wouldn't do anything to ruin the happiness they'd found.

But he would do what it took to keep Sybil safe. It's what Hannah would want.

"No," he said. "Pack what you need for a week or two and have Hiro fly you somewhere no one will think to look for you. You can give me his cell number and I'll call you as soon as I have any updates on the situation."

"But I—"

"I know you want to help find Hannah," Jackson interrupted gently. "But the people who have taken her are dangerous. Hannah loves you more than anything. If I brought you into a situation that would put your life in danger, she would have my balls for breakfast."

Sybil's laugh ended in a soft sob. "Sounds like you know her well. Most people think she's a pushover. They don't see how strong she really is."

"I see her," Jackson said roughly. "And I love her and I swear to you I will get her back or die trying."

"Don't die," Sybil said. "There's been enough death and Hannah needs you. She loves you very much, too, Jackson. And I'm sure she knows you're doing everything you can to reach her."

"I hope so," he said, falling silent as Sybil gave him Hiro's familiar number and he pretended to write it down.

He hoped that Hannah believed he loved her. Or that he'd at least have the chance to explain that he hadn't given the kill order she must have seen on his phone.

He didn't care enough about Harley to want to kill her. Not anymore. His hate had faded to a two-dimensional emotion, one that could be folded and put away in a box inside of him and left to quietly decompose. The only passion he felt now was for Hannah, for her safety, her love, and the chance to build a life with the woman who had made him believe in miracles.

She was his miracle, his savior, his heart, and he was going to find her. He couldn't be too late. He couldn't have come so far out of the darkness only to lose his light.

LILI VALENTE

CHAPTER THREE

Hannah

The first thing Hannah felt was the sun warm on her face, then the cool breeze blowing across her bare arms and the gentle rocking of the boat beneath her.

They were lovely, lulling sensations, but none of them were the source of the desire pooling in her belly, making her blood feel hot and sticky. The source was the tongue swirling around her belly button, sending sizzles of awareness rushing through her and setting a hungry pulse to throbbing between her legs.

"Hmm…" She hummed lazily, opening her eyes to see Jackson's dark head bent over her stomach as his mouth made love to her navel with a singular focus that made her nipples bead tight beneath her damp bikini top.

"Are you finally awake?" he asked, his voice vibrating against her sun-warmed skin.

"I didn't know the belly button was an erogenous zone," she answered, reaching down to thread her fingers through his thick hair.

She loved his hair. Its softness, its sealskin color, the way it slid silkily through her fingers unless she fisted it in her hand and hung on for dear life.

"Silly woman." His tongue thrust deeper into the soft flesh, summoning an answering twinge low in her body. "In the right hands, all of your zones are erogenous zones."

She bit her lip, breath catching as Jackson's hand smoothed up the inside of her thigh. "Is that right?"

"Take your clavicle for example." Jackson kissed his way up through the valley between her breasts to the skin just below her neck. He kissed the place where her throat became her collarbone before letting his tongue trace a path across it to her shoulder. "If I wanted to, I could make you come just from kissing you here, again and again."

"Fascinating," she said with mock awe as she shivered, feeling his tongue in a hundred different places as he traced a line back the way he'd come.

He hadn't kissed her in any of the ways she usually associated with making love, but she was already wet and aching for him. Despite a healthy anti-foot-fetish, if Jackson told her that he could make her come from nibbling on her toes, she would believe him.

But that didn't mean it wasn't fun to tease...

"But I have to confess I have doubts about clavicle-induced orgasms," she said, as his tongue circled the hollow at the base of her throat, making her already tight nipples sting with the need for contact. "Are you sure you aren't being hyperbolic, Mr. Hawke?"

"You know I hate that word." He nipped at her neck, the feel of his teeth against her skin ratcheting her desire up another notch. "I'm many things, sunshine, but I'm not a liar."

"Hyperbole isn't a lie." She fought the urge to squirm as he turned his attention to the other side of her collarbone and fresh heat pooled between her legs. "It's an exaggerated statement never intended to be taken literally."

"I appreciate the grammar lesson," he said, dryly. "But I wasn't exaggerating. Do you want me to prove it?"

"No," she said, tightening her grip in his hair. "I'd rather you fuck me, sir. If that's all right with you."

He laughed softly as he moved on top of her, spreading her legs with a nudge of his knee before settling between them, pinning her against the warm wood of the deck. "I think I could be persuaded to fuck you. If you're a good girl."

"Or a bad one?" She lifted her hips,

grinding into the hard, hot ridge of his cock, still trapped behind his swim trunks.

He cursed against her mouth as their lips met in a long, slow, sultry kiss. "Either works for me. Choose your own adventure, sunshine, but choose quickly or I'll choose for you."

"I'll be good, but I want it a little rough," she whispered, a thrill zipping through her as the words left her lips. "I can't stop thinking about last night when you had your hand in my hair. It made me so wet, sir."

"Then roll over." Jackson pulled away, his volume dropping, the way it did when they started a scene.

It was his "I'm in charge now" voice, the one that held such incredible power over her body that she suspected there would come a day when he would be able to make her come with his voice alone, no touch required. "Now, Hannah. Don't make me ask again."

"Yes, sir." She hurried to obey his command, rolling over onto her stomach before pushing up onto her hands and knees on the beach towel she'd spread on the deck after their swim, her thighs already trembling with anticipation.

But she should have known Jackson wouldn't want her in the same position as last night.

Her love wasn't only sweetly skilled and wonderfully wicked; he was creative.

"Swimsuit off and on your belly. Arms in front of you and legs spread."

As she hurried to obey, Jackson crossed to the other side of the boat, collecting something from the banquet where they'd had lunch before returning to her side.

"Lift your hips," he said.

Hannah curved her spine and Jackson slipped a small pillow from the seating area beneath her pelvis before setting a hand on her bottom, signaling for her to relax.

"Now you're ready." He pressed a kiss to her shoulder as he tied her wrists in front of her with her discarded sarong. "Now I'll be able to fuck you without leaving bruises on your pretty hip bones."

"I don't mind a bruise or two." Hannah held her breath as he moved behind her, holding himself up in a push-up position, hovering close enough for her to feel the heat of his body, but not the brush of his skin against hers.

"Well, I do." He kissed her other shoulder, making her ache for the feel of his weight settling on top of her.

But he held himself away, taking his time trailing kisses up the back of her neck. "No bruises today. You're too beautiful. All your sun-warmed skin and that white tan line on your ass. I've been dying to get you out of your swimsuit all day."

"You should have said something sooner," she whispered, shivering as his fingers wrapped gently around her throat, urging her to tilt her head back and push up on her forearms. "There's no one around to see. We could have gone sailing naked."

"Sometimes delayed satisfaction is the best kind." His fingers trailed down her throat to skim the top of her breast. "Don't you think?"

"How are you holding yourself up with one arm?" she asked, breath coming faster as her nipples pulled tight, aching for his touch. "I want to feel you."

"I want to feel you, sir," he corrected, but there was amusement in his voice. "And the answer is skill, sunshine. Patience and skill. Arch your back more. Yes, like that. Perfect."

He captured her nipple between his fingertips, pinching with the barest teasing pressure. "Now I want you to hold absolutely still. Don't move, don't squirm those pretty hips, don't even let your shoulders rise and fall too fast as you breathe. Do you understand?"

"Yes, sir," she said, pressing her lips together as soon as the words left her mouth, sensing that obedience was going to be a battle.

Even with his warm fingers barely touching her nipple, it felt like her nerves were being set on fire. Electricity hummed from her sensitive tips to knot between her legs. As he transferred his attentions from one nipple to the other—continuing to hover above her body in a one-armed push-up position that she couldn't believe even *he* could sustain for this long—her clit swelled and the pulse between her thighs picked up speed.

"I love your breasts," Jackson whispered, kissing the place where her neck curved into her shoulder. "I love how your nipples get so tight for me."

Hannah squeezed her eyes shut and dug her teeth into her bottom lip, fighting to stay still as he pinched and teased her nipples and her breath came faster, making her stomach flutter against the towel beneath her.

"I love the sounds you make when I bite them," he said, trapping a mouthful of the top of her shoulder between his teeth and biting down, making her groan as a primal wave of lust rocketed through her.

"Yes, bite me again, sir," she whispered, her entire body beginning to tremble. "Please. Please bite me again."

"Not yet, sweetness," he said, returning his teasing attention to her breasts, plucking first one nipple and then the other until it was pure hell not to move and a soft whimper escaped her lips. "You're doing so well, but I know you can give me more. Spread your legs wider."

She obeyed, so relieved to be granted permission to move, even just a little bit, that she danced a few feet away from the razor's edge, regaining enough control that she was able to remain still when Jackson brought the tip of his cock to her entrance.

It rested lightly at her opening, enough for her to feel how hot and hard he was, but not enough to grant her even the slightest bit of relief.

All she wanted was to lift her hips and shove backward, impaling herself on his erection.

She wanted it so badly her inner walls pulsed and her body gushed wetness onto the blunt head of his cock, desperate to ease his way. But instead of pushing forward, he rocked his hips slowly from side to side, teasing first one side of her opening and then the other, while his fingers continued to twist and pluck at her nipples and Hannah slowly went out of her mind.

"God, please, Jackson," she panted, tears rising in her eyes as she fought the overwhelming urge to move. "Please, please,

please."

"Please, what," he demanded, tongue teasing back and forth across the place where he'd bitten her, where she was dying for him to bite her again. "And please, who?"

"Please fuck me, sir," she practically snarled, so desperate for relief she couldn't decide if she loved him or hated him. "Please, I can't take any more. I can't."

"Yes, you can." The strain in his voice indicating that he was nearing the edge of his own control was the only thing that kept her from breaking.

"Just another minute, sunshine," he continued. "You can do anything for one more minute. Sixty, fifty-nine, fifty-eight…"

As he counted down his touch grew rougher, harder, until he was twisting her nipples in painful, blissful circles and she was panting for breath and making desperate, unfeminine sounds low in her throat.

But she didn't care. She was beyond caring about what Jackson thought of her. All she cared about was relief from the pressure mounting to a previously unfathomable peak inside of her. She was so high on lust there was no air to breathe.

Higher, higher, he took her until the world spun and her head felt too light for her body.

For a moment, she was afraid she would suffocate on her own desire and pass out before Jackson decided to end his erotic torture.

But then he bit her again, hard enough to send pain flashing through her nerve endings, and dropped his hips, shoving all the way to the end of her.

Her cry of pain became a high-pitched keen as Jackson wrapped a bracing arm around her ribs and slammed all the way to the end of her, triggering an orgasm so intense it was like an atom bomb had been detonated in her core.

Hannah clawed at the deck beneath her as the world went white and she was blinded by pleasure. Euphoria spread from her center out to bathe every inch of her body in bliss, the release so sweet that pleasure became pain and then swung back around to pleasure again in a seemingly endless feedback loop while

Jackson fucked her so hard she felt him everywhere.

Everywhere.

In her belly, in her ribs, in her throat, filling her up until there was no place he hadn't touched and there was no awareness of what was his and what was hers.

There was only pulse and throb, hunger and satisfaction, love and the communion of two hearts beating in perfect harmony.

Hannah was dimly aware of Jackson finding release and rolling onto his back, pulling her on top of him while he freed her hands, but she was still too lost in that other world they'd found together to pay too much attention to her body. She was at ten thousand feet, soaring weightless, not certain she would ever come down.

She had no idea how long she lay on top of him, catching her breath, only that when she finally opened her eyes the blue sky was stained with sunset light and the sea air had grown cooler.

"I wonder if that's what heroin is like," she rasped, her voice rough.

"If so, no wonder it's so hard to quit." Jackson's fingers played gently up and down her stomach. "How do you do it?"

"Do what?" She turned her head, meeting his eyes over her shoulder, her heart flipping when she saw the vulnerable, open expression on his face.

"Make me want you more every day?"

She lifted her hand, cupping his scruffy cheek in her hand. "Dark magic."

He smiled, and her flipping heart turned a cartwheel. "I believe it. There's no other explanation."

But there was another explanation.

It was love. Once-in-a-lifetime, only-gets-better, love-you-more-every-day-until-they-put-me-in-the-ground love. She'd known that for a while now and someday soon, Jackson would know it, too.

She didn't doubt it, not even on those mornings when he stayed in his room until well after breakfast, hiding from her after a night when close had become too close for his comfort.

There would come a day when he would

realize that there was no need to hide and nothing to be afraid of.

He was safe with her. He could let his guard down and be the man he truly was, the man who was as sweet as he was Dominant, as gentle as he was controlling. She would never take his love for granted or betray his trust.

Never.

No matter what.

"No matter what," she said aloud, her brows drawing together as something ugly whispered through her subconscious.

It was like a foul smell drifting through the air, familiar, but horrible, something she knew she didn't want to recognize.

Once she named it, there would be no denying the existence of the filth smeared across the walls or the body rotting beneath the floor.

Once she remembered, she would never forget again.

"What's wrong?" Jackson asked, his voice going deep and dangerous as the orange sky darkened, black and blue creeping in to bruise the undersides of the clouds. "Cat got your tongue, Harley?"

Before she could reply, or tell him that she wasn't Harley, Jackson's hands were back around her throat.

But this time, his touch wasn't gentle. His fingers tightened like a vice and pain blossomed through her forehead, the pressure building suddenly, fiercely, until it felt like her eyes would burst from their sockets.

Panicked, she clawed at Jackson's arms, desperate for breath, but his grip only tightened.

"You're going to die, Harley," he growled against her throat as the world went black. "I will end you if it's the last thing I do."

CHAPTER FOUR

Hannah

Hannah woke with a startled groan, hands flying to her neck.

She gasped for breath, her throat still tight from the terror of the beautiful memory turned nightmare.

She swallowed slowly and blinked, willing herself to remember the way that day on the boat had really ended, with her and Jackson sailing home under the stars. She'd snuggled in his lap as he'd steered with one arm wrapped around her waist, holding her close to him with a gentleness that made it clear that she was precious to him.

Her heartbeat was nearly under control when the world pitched. A moment later, the plane touched down with a rough bump.

Startled, Hannah turned to look out the window, where pale light glowed on the horizon and unfamiliar palm trees—more sparse and scrubby than the ones back home—streaked past the window.

For a moment, she couldn't remember where she was, but then it all came rushing back—Adam in the doorway, the miracle of learning that her sister was alive, the pain of realizing Jackson planned to kill Harley, and then the terror of grasping that she had much bigger problems than a broken heart.

She had been kidnapped by Jackson's father and he was going to kill her. Or Harley. But first, he was going to make her father choose between the daughters he'd sacrificed so much to protect.

Depending on how things played out, this could be the last sunrise Hannah would ever see.

No. He won't get away with this.

You'll find a way out and you'll take Harley with you.

Hannah swallowed hard.

Ignoring the lingering taste of her own sickness in her mouth and the acrid scent rising from the blanket she'd thrown over the puddle of vomit, she glanced around the cabin. Jackson's father was nowhere in sight.

He and Adam must both be in the cockpit, landing the plane, which meant she was alone for a few precious moments and she meant to make the most of them.

Flicking open her seatbelt, she lurched out of her seat, clinging to the back of the seat behind her, fighting the drag of the g-force as the plane continued to decelerate. She pulled her way to the rear of the cabin to a large desk that occupied most of the space near the bathroom and snatched the slim gray phone from its cradle, sagging with relief when she heard the buzz of the dial tone.

She'd noticed the phone last night, but under Ian's watchful eye there had been no opportunity to attempt a call for help. Now, she had at least a minute or two before the men finished landing the plane.

Hopefully, it would be enough.

Quickly, she punched in the familiar phone number and waited with held breath as soft clicks drifted from the receiver, signaling that the call was trying to connect. She rubbed the sleep from her eyes with her free hand as her brain sparked and hummed, waking up fast as adrenaline dumped into her system.

She couldn't believe she'd fallen asleep with Ian sitting across from her, watching her like an animal he couldn't wait to slaughter. It must have been a defense mechanism, a way to cope with the stress induced by sharing air with a predator.

Whatever kindness Jackson possessed, he'd clearly inherited it from his mother.

Based on their few hours of acquaintance, Hannah was willing to bet that Ian Hawke was a prototypical psychopath—a creature utterly without empathy or remorse—but she didn't intend to stick around to confirm her diagnosis.

She was going to get away from Ian, even if she had to reach out to one monster to be saved from another.

She couldn't believe that Jackson had anything to do with her abduction. The tortured note in his voice as he'd called after her had been too real.

Finally, after several more clicks and a long, vibrating silence that made Hannah's stomach sink with dread, the phone rang just as the plane slowed to cruising speed. Hannah's fingers tightened around the receiver as she spun to look over her shoulder, praying that Jackson would answer before his father came back through the cockpit's door.

He picked up halfway through the second ring. "Who is this?"

Unexpected tears surged into Hannah's eyes, her throat locking tight as a wave of relief and longing swept through her.

No matter what he'd done, it was so fucking good to hear Jackson's voice.

"It's Hannah, but I don't have much time,"

she said, sucking in a panicked breath. "Adam is working for your father. I'm on his private plane right now. We just landed somewhere with palm trees, but a long way from Tahiti. We were flying all night and the sun is just now coming up."

"I'm coming for you. Can you see anything outside?" Jackson asked, getting right down to business though the strain in his voice made it clear he was worried about her.

He was fine with killing Harley, but it seemed he still cared whether she lived or died.

"Are there any identifying landmarks," he continued, "or an airfield name or—"

"Nothing. Just the palm trees." Hannah leaned down to stare out one of the rear windows as the plane made a slight turn to the left, revealing a stunning view of the ocean and a tiny island off the coast.

"No, wait," she said. "There's a little island next to the airstrip. It has a beach, a small dock, and bright red hammocks hanging in the trees. There's no one there now, but it looks like some kind of tourist destination.

Maybe that will help?"

"Maybe, but keep looking, and if we're disconnected know that I'm close," Jackson said, making Hannah's knees go weak with relief. "The last satellite image had you near the Florida Keys. We're only a couple of hours behind you. We'll figure out where you've landed and I'll get to you before he hurts you. I promise, Hannah. I swear it on my life. Just hold on."

"I will, but hurry," she said, sniffing hard as tears filled her eyes. "He's going to kill me, Jackson. Me or Harley. I know you don't care about her, but I—"

"No, you don't understand, baby. I never—"

With a click and an ominous sounding whine, the line went dead.

Stifling a panicked cry, Hannah jabbed at the switch hook, trying to get back to an open line and call him back.

She needed to hear his voice again. She needed him to finish what he'd been about to say. Maybe there had been some kind of horrible misunderstanding. Maybe he hadn't betrayed her, maybe there was—

"Just like Romeo and Juliet." A low voice from behind her broke into her panicked thoughts.

Hannah whirled to see Ian seated on the small sofa, his long legs crossed.

"Two households, alike in dignity," he continued, a smirk on his face. "An ancient grudge that lingers on, souring the hearts of both young and old…"

"You have no heart," Hannah whispered, letting the phone slip from her hand. "Jackson told me all about you."

Ian's brows rose. "I doubt *all* about. My son and I have never been close. I don't tell him my secrets." He lifted one shoulder and let it fall. "I don't tell anyone my secrets. That's the best way to keep them, don't you think?"

Hannah leaned against the desk as the plane continued to taxi toward some unknown destination, wishing she had tried to open the cabin door when she had the chance.

Now Ian sat between her and a possible

break for freedom and there was no chance of overpowering him. He looked like he was well into his sixties but was in excellent physical condition, nearly as powerful and intimidating as his son.

"Unfortunately, Jackson is closer to sorting out our destination than I anticipated," Ian continued. "I'd hoped my contacts at the Titan group would be able to steer him in the wrong direction, but it looks like he's decided to take matters into his own hands."

Hannah frowned. "The Titan group. Those are the people who texted Jackson the picture of Harley."

"Yes." Ian stood, shaking out the front of his gray slacks. "I asked Alexander to wait to send the image until the timing was right for Adam to extract you from the island."

"Adam's the one who sent the text telling them to kill Harley, not Jackson," she said, feeling like a fool.

She should have questioned the text, and Jackson's right-hand man, the moment she saw the kill order.

Deep down, she'd known that wasn't who

Jackson was. Not anymore.

He loved her—madly maybe, but truly. She should have trusted in that love instead of letting fear send her running into the hands of her enemies.

Ian nodded, amusement curving the edges of his mouth.

"Trust is such a fragile thing, isn't it," he said as if reading her mind. "So hard to gain and so easy to lose. You didn't even stop to think he might have been framed, did you?"

Hannah dropped her gaze to the floor without bothering to reply.

Obviously she hadn't stopped to think or she wouldn't be here right now.

"It's all right," Ian continued. "If anyone should understand how hard it can be to build trust, it's my son. I'm sure he'll forgive you. Perhaps one day you two will be together again. Assuming you're the sister lucky enough to walk away."

"You don't get to do this." Hannah glared at him, rage sweeping through her like a hot wind, banishing her fear. "You don't get to decide whether Harley or I live or die!"

"But I do, sweetheart," Ian said breezily, as the plane pulled to a stop. "And there's nothing you or my son can do to stop me. By the time Jackson finds out where we are, one of you will already be dead."

Adam emerged from the cockpit and Ian turned to him with a wave of one hand.

"Escort Hannah to see her sister and then meet me in my office," he said. "We're moving up the timetable. I want to have this finished before lunch."

Hannah balked at the words.

The man wanted to get the murdering out of the way so he could enjoy his noon meal. If she'd had any doubts that Ian was a psychopath—or beyond the reach of appeals for mercy—they would have vanished at that moment.

A wave of sickness tightened her throat, but there wasn't anything left in her stomach. She hadn't had so much as a drink of water since boarding the aircraft. She'd been too traumatized to think about asking for food or drink.

But now, as Adam led her from the plane

and across a wild, overgrown lawn toward a mansion that made her father's look reserved in comparison, she wished she'd at least asked for a bottle of water. She didn't want to die with the taste of her own sickness ripe in her mouth.

She didn't want to face down a gun or a knife or whatever Ian had planned for her feeling weak with thirst.

If she was going to die, she wanted to die with dignity, standing tall and strong, meeting Ian Hawke's cold gaze and letting him know that he hadn't won. He could take her life, but he would never break her spirit.

The only person who could ever break her was Jackson because she'd loved him too much to hold him at a safe distance.

Loved him so much you turned on him at the first sign of trouble.

What kind of love is that?

You should have talked to him, the way you were always insisting he talk to you.

Her inner voice was right, but there was nothing she could do about it now.

As Adam led her into the tomblike silence

of the giant home and up a curving staircase, Hannah just hoped she would live long enough to learn from her mistake.

CHAPTER FIVE

Jackson

Somewhere over Mexico, minutes after the line went dead without him knowing if Hannah had heard that he hadn't given the kill order, Jackson forced himself to lie down. He was so wired and scared for Hannah that he knew rest wouldn't come easy, but he had to try.

He couldn't face his father burned out and

exhausted.

Ian was always five steps ahead of everyone, but Jackson wasn't the same relatively naïve kid he'd been growing up in his father's house. He'd learned his share about outthinking his enemies, and this time he was fighting for something more important than a shipment of illegal arms or a good price on his latest black market investment.

He was fighting for Hannah's life, and her sister's, too.

If his father killed Harley, Hannah would never forgive him. He had to make this right. He had to think six steps ahead and be waiting for Ian when he turned the corner.

He was off to a good start—he'd already learned that Stewart Mason, his father, and Alexander Titan, of the Titan Group, had served in the same squadron in Vietnam. Therefore, he also knew that he couldn't trust the intelligence he'd received from the Titan Group or hold on to his previously held beliefs about his father.

The realization had led him to dig beneath the surface, deeper into Ian's past.

Turns out, Ian Hawke wasn't the last living member of a Texas oil family, the way he'd led everyone—including his wife—to believe. He was a thug who had grown up in a Chicago slum and, before he was drafted, been well on his way to living a life of crime.

Yes, he'd been awarded his share of medals during his service, but he'd also been written up for insubordination dozens of times. If he'd been serving at any other time than during the least popular war in modern history, Ian would have been discharged before his second tour of duty.

Armed with nothing more than an Internet connection and better-than-average hacking skills, Jackson had unearthed a dozen skeletons in his father's closet. It made him ashamed of himself for not looking behind the mask years ago. But Ian was good at pretending to be something he wasn't.

He was also good at eliminating possible threats before they became *probable* ones.

Jackson had to assume that Ian would know he was on his way so they'd made plans to land at an airstrip on the opposite side of the island from the mansion his father's subsidiary company had purchased last June. Jackson wanted to keep the news of their arrival from Ian as long as possible and hopefully gain entrance to the house unnoticed.

He refused to think about what would happen if his guess were wrong and the home was empty. He wouldn't think about how much time that would waste or what might happen to Hannah while he was scrambling to locate whatever snake hole his father had crawled into.

He had to trust the intelligence he'd gathered and have faith that he was on track to saving the woman he loved.

But faith was harder to hold on to when he was alone. With Hannah, it had begun to feel natural to wake up in the morning believing he would continue to become a better man, one worthy of her good heart.

Now, as he drifted into a fitful sleep, he wasn't sure what he believed. The only thing he knew for sure was that if his father killed Hannah, hers would be the last murder he would live to commit.

Jackson slept, dreaming of a sweltering battlefield where he hunted his father through a blood-soaked jungle and down a hole in the ground that smelled of death and decay. He dreamt of screams and pain and rats that burrowed into the bodies of wounded men, and he woke covered in sweat in time to hear Dominic's half of an ominous sounding phone call.

"Tell him to stall as long as he can," Dom said, his troubled gaze trained out the window. "We'll land in half an hour and be at the house not long after. If he can put it off for even an hour, we'll be there in time to intervene."

Dominic sighed, shaking his head at whatever the person on the other line was saying. "I don't know, Peter. I'll figure something out. You just make sure Mr. Mason doesn't make contact until he absolutely has to."

He ended the call with a jab of his thumb and tossed the phone angrily onto the seat beside him, catching Jackson's eye as he moved. "You're awake," he said, the frustration fading from his features, replaced by a carefully neutral expression that made Jackson wish he were on this plane with someone he knew he could trust.

"I am." Jackson sat up, running a hand through his hair as he pushed the light blanket to the end of the couch. "Who's stalling and why?"

"Your father made contact with Mr. Mason and told him he had the girls." Dominic plucked his phone from the seat, tucking it into his front pocket. "Stewart was told to get to a secure computer and prepare for a Skype call in twenty minutes."

Jackson's hands balled into fists. "Do you think Hannah was right? Is Ian going to make Mason choose between them?"

"I don't know," Dom said, the muscle in his jaw leaping. "But nothing good is going to come from taking that call. The longer Stewart can put it off, the better. My associate, Peter, is trying to find someone in our network close enough to Key West to offer backup, but there's a good chance they won't get there in time. We may be on our own."

"We should plan on it," Jackson said. "There are already enough unknown variables. We shouldn't go in counting on someone who won't be there."

Dom turned, pinning Jackson with a hard look. "And what about you? Can I count on you?"

Jackson's expression darkened, but Dom pushed on before he could respond.

"I'm not trying to be an asshole. I believe you care about Hannah, but this man is your father. If it comes down to a choice between him and her, are you going to be able to do what needs to be done?"

"Hannah is all that matters," Jackson said, holding the other man's gaze. "I will do whatever it takes to get her out of there alive."

"And Harley?" Dom pushed. "Because I'm not going in to save just one of them."

"If I can save Harley without risking Hannah, I will. If not, I won't," Jackson answered honestly. "Like I said, Hannah is what matters. I'd rather spend the rest of my life begging her forgiveness for failing to save her sister than hating myself for letting Hannah die."

Dom studied him for a long moment, doubt clear in his dark eyes. "The rest of your life, huh? You're serious about that?"

Jackson fought the urge to snap that it was none of Dom's business what he was or wasn't serious about. Like it or not, Dominic was the only ally he had, and they didn't have time to waste bickering amongst themselves. "I am. If she'll have me."

"You don't think you'll get bored," Dom said in a cold voice. "Once you've smacked her around for a year or two."

Jackson's jaw clenched, but he refused to move—or speak—until the wave of anger summoned by the other man's words had faded. "The things Hannah and I do together are consensual. Not that it's any of your business, but more often than not, she's the one who instigates a scene."

"Right," the other man sneered.

"For the past month, she remained on the island with me of her own free will," Jackson snapped, unable to believe he was being forced to waste time justifying his and Hannah's sexual preferences when her life was in danger. "Clearly, she doesn't feel that she's being abused."

"Yeah, well things can get confusing for victims," Dom shot back. "I've seen it before. They get beaten down so low they confuse the absence of pain with pleasure."

Jackson leaned forward, no longer making any attempt to hide the heat in his gaze. "Hannah is one of the strongest people I've ever met. I haven't beaten her down; she's lifted me up. I am not a perfect man, far from it, but she makes me want to be. I love her and I would die before I would willingly hurt her again."

He paused, making sure Dom was paying attention before he added in a harder voice, "You can choose to believe that or not, but don't you dare call her a victim again. You're insulting her strength and intelligence, and not much makes me angrier than that."

Dominic's eyes narrowed, but after a moment, he shrugged. "Fine. I'll keep my mouth shut. And assuming we get them both out alive and Hannah chooses to stay with you, I won't try to interfere."

"Good."

"But I won't sit by and watch it happen, either." Dom pushed his armrest up with a rough shove. "Assuming she's still in need of protection, I'll ask for someone else to be assigned to her detail. I can't watch a sweet woman like her flush her life and free will away. It's too fucking depressing."

Jackson sighed, the fight slowly going out of him.

Dom was obviously one of the many people in the world who would never understand the kind of relationship he and Hannah both craved. There were few people who did, which had always made it hard for him to imagine finding happily ever after.

Even back before Harley had made sure romance was the last thing on his mind, he'd been cautious when it came to love. He'd learned from experience that he wasn't going to find long-term happiness with a vanilla woman, no matter how beautiful, funny, or likable she might be. He craved the thrill of Domination too much, needed the rush when his top came out to play with a woman who could handle everything he could dish out.

But she needed to truly be able to handle and *enjoy* it, to be tough enough to meet him as an equal in the game.

That's what so many people didn't understand: that a submissive can be every bit as strong as her Dom. Her strength simply manifests in different ways. He had never met that uniquely resilient, yet submissive, woman in his younger years, and even Harley had only pretended to want the same things he wanted. He had never believed he could find that forever kind of happiness with a woman until now.

Hannah was one in a million, the strong, sensitive, beautiful, clever, kinky-as-hell lover he hadn't believed existed until she'd swept into his life. She was his hurricane and his touchstone. She was an endless adventure and the home he never thought he'd find.

She was…everything, but he hadn't told her all the things that were in his heart. And now, if he failed her today, she might never know that she was the answer to everything, even the questions he'd been too stupid to ask.

"Listen," Jackson said, his voice rough with emotion. "You do what you have to do. But right now we need to focus on saving two women's lives. Can we put aside our differences and concentrate on that? Because I need Hannah alive a hell of a lot more than I need you to agree with my lifestyle choices."

Dom's nostrils flared, but after only a moment he nodded. "There will be a car waiting for us at the airstrip and I found a blueprint of the house." He reached into his pocket, pulling out his phone. "I've marked the places where I think they're likely to keep prisoners and where we've got the best chance of getting in undetected. But why don't you do a once over, too. See if there's anything I've overlooked."

Jackson took the phone from Dom's outstretched hand, surprised to find their argument had made him more confident in depending on the other man for backup.

Stewart Mason could be paying this man more money than God for all he knew, but money couldn't buy loyalty. Adam had taught him that. Knowing that Dominic cared about Hannah enough to start an argument with someone nearly twice his size made him trust that the man would do whatever he could to get Hannah to safety.

Now they just had to get there in time for him to eliminate the threat to Hannah once and for all.

Dom didn't have to worry; Jackson was ready to do what needed to be done.

As long as Ian Hawke walked the earth, Hannah would never be safe. It didn't matter that her father had likely committed a crime worthy of a heaping helping of vengeance. The moment Ian had started killing innocent people in his quest for revenge, he'd proven that it was time for him to be put down.

It wasn't something Jackson was eager to do, but he had no other option. As he'd told Dominic, Hannah was his first priority and he would do whatever it took—including killing his own father—to keep her safe.

CHAPTER SIX

Hannah

Hannah was too busy memorizing the layout of the house and looking for possible avenues of escape to have time to anticipate what it would be like to see Harley for the first time in six years.

When Adam paused to shove open the bolt on the door at the end of a long hallway on the third floor, she was watching the mechanism slide and wondering if there was a way to force it open from the inside. She wasn't thinking about reunions or the fact that somewhere beyond the door her long lost sister was waiting for her.

And then, Adam pushed her over the threshold and suddenly she was inside with the door closing behind her, staring into the eyes of her missing piece.

Hannah's breath caught and pain flooded through her, leaving her entire body feeling bruised.

There she was, rising slowly from the window seat on the other side of the room, the sister who had once been like a part of her own body and soul. With her hair bleached blonde and her skin a pale, creamy shade that bore testament to how little time she must spend in the sun, Harley looked different, but there was no doubt it was her.

Hannah held her sister's troubled gaze, her gut twisting with love and regret and a fierce, bittersweet nostalgia, but the familiar rush of affinity never came.

This woman was no longer her other half.

Jackson was her other half, and if she hadn't come into his life when she did, the man she loved would never have found his way out of the hell Harley had consigned him to.

"I'm sorry," Harley said, her eyes shining. "I'm so sorry, Hannah."

"For what?" Hannah asked, not taking another step into the room, not ready to get any closer to Harley than she was already.

"I should have found a way to let you know I was alive." Harley's lashes swept down, sending the tears in her eyes sliding down her pale cheeks. "Dad told me I couldn't because it would put you in danger. But I knew losing me would kill you, the way losing you killed me. I've missed you so much, moo."

She pulled in a breath, pressing her lips together as she swiped the wet from her face with her fist. "Please tell me you'll forgive me. If I die here, I don't want to die with you hating me."

"I don't hate you." The lump in Hannah's throat grew a size or three, making it hard to swallow, but her eyes remained dry. "Though I should. I know what you did to Jackson Hawke."

Harley blinked, her brow furrowing as if she were having trouble placing the name.

"Don't you dare pretend you don't remember him," Hannah said, her hands balling into fists at her sides. "Don't you dare because then I will hate you. Forever. No going back."

Her sister swallowed, her thin throat working. "No, I do remember, I just… I wasn't expecting to hear that name. Especially from you."

"I understand." Hannah's lips curved in what she was certain was an ugly smile. "I wasn't expecting Jackson to come looking for me, either. I was totally unprepared. So was he. He had no idea you had a twin sister. He thought I was you, the woman who had betrayed him and ruined his life."

"Oh my God," Harley whispered, a trembling hand coming to cover her lips. "Are you okay? Did he hurt you?"

"Not as much as you have," Hannah said,

knowing now wasn't the time to go into how she'd ended up on a private island with Jackson or how long she'd felt compelled to pretend to be her sister.

They didn't have time to waste catching up; they had to find a way out.

But she had to know one thing first. "Why did you do it?" she asked. "Why did you frame an innocent man?"

Harley crossed her arms at her chest, pulling the thin gray sweater she wore tighter across her shoulders. "God, Hannah, I don't know. It was all so messed up. If I could go back and undo it, I would. I swear I would."

"That's not what I asked," Hannah said, her voice cold. "I want to know *why*. Did you even have a reason, or did destroying a man just seem like a fun way to spend the summer?"

Her sister flinched. "I know I deserve that, but I promise you, I'm not that person anymore. I hope I have time to prove that to you and to prove how sorry I am." She wiped the last of her tears away with her sleeve. "As far as the other, I convinced myself ruining

Jackson was fair play. An eye for an eye, someone I loved for someone he loved."

Hannah frowned. "Jackson loved *you*. I don't—"

"Not Jackson, his father," she said. "Ian Hawke was the one who took Mom away, Hannah. He's the one who broke her."

"What?" Hannah frowned but understanding clicked into place before Harley could respond. "You mean he was the man Mom had the affair with? When we were kids?"

She nodded. "Now I know seducing Mom was all part of Ian's obsession with evening an old score with Daddy, but I didn't back then."

Harley paced toward the two leather couches in the middle of the room and stared into the empty fireplace. "I just knew he was the man who'd ruined our family so...I decided to ruin his."

Hannah shook her head. "That isn't justice, Harley. Jackson was innocent. Completely. At least Mom went with Ian of her own free will, Jackson was just—"

"I know that," Harley said, her pitch rising

as she spun to face Hannah. "Believe me, Hannah, I know. I fucked everything up and ruined people's lives and proved I was every bit as evil as that man who plans to kill one of us."

She stepped closer, until only a few feet separated them, before continuing in a softer voice, "And I swear I would give my own life if it would make it all right again, but it won't. The only thing I can do is move forward trying not to do any more harm."

Her tongue slipped out to dampen her lips. "And that's what I've done and why I have an enormous favor to ask you."

"A favor." Hannah's breath huffed out. "Considering I might die today, Harley, I don't think I'm in a place to make promises."

"You're not going to die," Harley said, a resigned look in her bloodshot eyes. "I've had a few days to think about this and I seriously don't see Daddy choosing me. He knows you deserve mercy more than I do, and I think a part of him would like an excuse to bring Jasper to live with him."

Hannah's brow furrowed, but Harley

pushed on before she could imagine who Jasper might be.

"He thinks it would be better with a boy, easier, or something, but he's wrong." Harley's lip curled. "He'd get tired of Jasper the same way he got tired of us, and I can't stand for my son to grow up that way."

Hannah leaned back against the door, her knees suddenly unsteady.

Harley had a child?

A little boy, who would be left without a mother if their father chose to spare Hannah's life instead of hers?

Harley threaded her hands together in front of her. "That's why I want you to take him, Hannah. I don't know if you have kids, but I truly—"

"I don't," Hannah said, the admission sending another wave of pain through her chest.

Her dreams of love and family had disappeared along with her other dreams, on the day her sister had died and she'd learned she was a hunted woman.

But they'd come back. With Jackson, for a

stolen moment in time that was likely all she would ever know of romantic love.

Harley's expression softened. "Well, I have no doubt you'll be an amazing mother. And I know you would love Jasper like he was yours. He's such a good, smart, sweet kid, just like you were when we were little. And I've told him all about you so he won't be shocked to see someone who looks like me."

She paused, tears rising in her eyes again before she added, "I think it would give him comfort, really. And maybe someday he wouldn't even remember the difference between his first mom and his second one."

"Jesus." Hannah closed her eyes, sagging more heavily against the door. Her thoughts raced even as her pulse slowed until her hands felt like lumps of ice at the ends of her arms.

"Please, Hannah," Harley begged, her voice even closer now. "I know it's a lot to take in, but—"

"Dad's not going to choose me," Hannah said, forcing her eyes open. She couldn't fall apart now, not when Harley had basically confirmed that the only way she was getting out of here alive was if she managed to escape before Adam returned. "He won't take Jasper's mother away from him. If it comes down to making a choice, you'll be the one walking away from this."

Harley shook her head. "Have you forgotten who our father is? He's not going to care about taking me away from Jasper. He'll convince himself it's for the best. If I'm dead, then Jasper won't have to hide. He'll be able to come back to the States and live like a prince and start kindergarten next fall where the kids speak English. It's everything Dad's wanted for the past five years."

For the past five years.

Hannah's gut churned as she quickly did the math. Harley's son was five years old, getting ready to start kindergarten, which meant she must have gotten pregnant that summer six years ago, which meant…

Jasper might be Jackson's.

Jackson could have a son.

It was a painful realization—she didn't want to think about Jackson having children with another woman, especially her sister—

but it was also a reason to love the little boy even more. Jasper might be more than her nephew; he might also be a piece of the man she loved.

"If something happens to you, I will take care of Jasper," Hannah promised, knowing it was the right decision as soon as the words left her lips. "I will love him like he's my own and do everything I can to give him a happy life."

Harley's shoulders sagged. "Thank you, moo. Thank you so much."

"But let's make sure nothing happens to you. Or to me," she said, motioning toward the window as she crossed the room. "How do things look outside? Are there guards who will notice two women climbing out a window?"

"I haven't seen any guards," Harley said, following her. "But there's nothing in here to use for a rope. I took the covers off the couch cushions and tried to tie them together, but the leather is too thick. And even if we could find a way to connect the pieces, they wouldn't reach far enough anyway. We're three stories off the ground."

Hannah opened the window, letting in the cool, but muggy, Florida winter air. She leaned forward to press her face against the screen, taking in the sheer drop down to the grass below.

There was nothing to hold on to and a fall from this far up would likely kill them. It would definitely leave them too hurt to run, and then they would end up right back where they were now.

But Harley was right, there was nothing in the room except bookshelves and the two leather couches, no bed sheets or clothes or anything else they could use to make a rope.

"But there are two of us now," Hannah murmured, gaze shifting left and right, trying to get a better idea of how far up they were.

The bottom floor had a vaulted ceiling—she'd noticed that on the way through the foyer to the stairs—but the next two floors seemed fairly standard sized.

She guessed they were about thirty feet up. Cut that number in half and one of them would have an excellent chance of surviving the drop without being any worse for wear.

She spun back to Harley, gaze skimming up and down as she took in her sister's clothing. The gray sweater wasn't very thick, but it looked strong. If they used the sweater to tie them to something heavy…

LILI VALENTE

CHAPTER SEVEN

Hannah

"Let me see your sweater," she said, holding out her hand.

Harley frowned, but obediently stripped off the sweater, revealing the tight gray tee shirt she wore beneath. It hugged her sister's torso, showcasing the ribs clearly visible beneath the fabric. She was even smaller than she used to be and her arms were thin, but soft, without a hint of muscle tone.

Still, Harley ought to have enough strength to hold on to Hannah's hands until it was time for her to drop to the ground.

"With my sweater, your dress, and my pants we've got maybe eight feet of rope," Harley said, proving she could still read Hannah's mind. "That still doesn't get us close enough to the ground and we'll be in our underwear when we run into the swamp."

"It's warm enough that exposure shouldn't be a problem and *we* won't be running anywhere," Hannah said, eyeing the couch and deciding it looked plenty heavy to serve her purpose. "*You're* going to be running into the swamp. We'll have eight feet of rope, five and a half feet of me once I tie the rope to my ankles, plus the length of our arms extended when we're holding hands. That will take you halfway to the ground. As long as you land with bent knees and roll across the grass you should be fine."

Harley's eyes widened. "And what happens to you after this circus trick?"

"I pull myself back up into the room,"

Hannah said, trying to act like the thought of dangling headfirst from a third story window didn't scare her half to death. "Ian wants to make Dad choose between us. He can't choose if I'm the only one here."

"What if he decides he doesn't care about making him choose," Harley said. "What if you fall?"

"I won't fall." She pushed on, talking over Harley's next argument. "And even if I do, I would rather die trying to escape than sit here waiting for Ian to kill one of us. Jackson's on his way to try to help, but his dad knows that and he's moved up the timetable. He could come for us any minute."

Harley blinked. "Jackson? Is on his way here?" She blinked again. "And he's coming to help *us*, not to help his father kill me?"

"It's a long story. I'll tell you as soon as we're somewhere safe," Hannah said, then added quickly, "but if you end up seeing Jackson before I do, tell him that I'm sorry I didn't trust him the way I should have. And that I love him and I always will."

Ignoring her sister's bug-eyed expression,

Hannah waved her toward the couch. "Come on. Help me move the couch. We'll secure the rope to the legs."

They had the couch pulled up beside the window, the screen shoved out onto the grass below, and had just finished ripping Harley's sweater into two long strips they were securing to the couch legs when the door opened.

Hannah turned to see Adam step inside, a gun in one hand and strips of long black fabric in the other.

CHAPTER EIGHT

Jackson

The driver who met them at the airstrip took them immediately to a marina nearby, where Mason's people had hired a speedboat for their use. Within ten minutes of touching down, they were on the water, racing around to the other side of the island, the salty wind in their faces making conversation impossible.

They were moving fast, but Jackson had no

idea if they would be fast enough. And when the hulking shadow of the mansion appeared around the next bend in the coast—a behemoth crouched on the top of a small rise, casting a dense blue shadow in the hazy winter light—the sight gave him little comfort.

The house looked abandoned, the windows dark and the yard overgrown.

His stomach clenched, but a moment later, the island Hannah had mentioned came into view on their right side. The snack bar was closed and the tiny dock empty, but red hammocks hung from the trees. A little farther along the coast, the palms on the opposite shore opened up, revealing a small private airstrip.

The plane with the red stripe down the nose sat at the end of it, only yards from the mansion's expansive lawn.

Dom motioned forward with two fingers, signaling that he was going to continue around to the other side of the house. They'd agreed that they shouldn't pull up to the beach within sight of the home—his father likely wouldn't be expecting them to have acquired a boat so quickly and wouldn't pay attention to a boat as long as it didn't stop near the house. Still, a part of Jackson wanted to take the wheel and aim them straight for the mansion's private dock.

Time was running out. He could feel it. The invisible tether connecting him to Hannah was being strained. Soon, it would snap. His gut kept screaming that he was minutes away from losing her and that every second counted.

The thought was barely through his head when a loud pop sounded from inside the home, echoing out across the water.

It was a gunshot, followed quickly by a second and a third.

CHAPTER NINE

Hannah

Adam blindfolded them before pushing them out into the hall. There, they were forced to fumble along with their hands on the wall and then to cling to the wooden handrail as they descended the stairs.

They were halfway to the first landing when Hannah heard Harley stumble behind her and turned to snap at Adam—

"We've already seen the house. I don't see the point in the blindfolds unless Ian's decided he wants us to die from falling down the stairs."

"Mr. Hawke wanted you blindfolded," Adam said in his usual low, disaffected voice.

"You always do what the Hawkes tell you to do?" Hannah asked, not afraid of the gun in Adam's hand. He wouldn't shoot them. Not until his master gave the signal, anyway.

"I do what the highest bidder tells me to do. Your father had the chance to pay up and make this go away, but he thought I was bluffing."

"We can pay," Harley piped up from behind her before Hannah could figure out what to make of Adam's claim.

If he were telling the truth, what did that mean for her and Harley? If Ian wanted money in addition to one of their lives, would their father give it? Stewart had always been generous when it came to his daughters, but maybe blackmail changed things.

"We've both got trust funds," Harley continued, "and I've made money on my artwork. Just let us go, and I'll give you everything."

"Too late for that," Adam said with a sniff. "But I'll do what I can to make it painless. Whichever one your father chooses."

"You're a fucking prince, Adam," Hannah sneered, shocked by how much she wanted to wrap her fingers around the man's neck and squeeze the life out of him with her bare hands.

He let forth a grunt of amusement, the closest she'd ever heard him come to laughter. "You used to be such a lady. Jackson's been a bad influence. Watch the last step."

"This is a mistake, Adam," Hannah said as she stepped down onto the ground floor, her bare feet tingling as they touched the cold, slick hardwood. "If you hurt me, Jackson will destroy you. You know I'm right. If I were you, I'd let us both go right now and run like hell."

"I'll be gone before he gets here. And as long as your dad chooses you, I should be okay." Adam took her arm. "He wanted the other one dead anyway."

Harley whimpered softly. Hannah reached back, fumbling until she found her sister's hand and squeezing tight, silently promising that she wouldn't let her die, not if she could do anything to stop it.

It didn't matter what Harley had done in the past. What mattered was that she had a little boy who needed his mother. Hannah didn't want to die, but she couldn't live with herself if she orphaned an innocent child.

She knew what that felt like, how devastating it was to lose the person you loved most in the world. There had been times, after her mother had first gone away, when she'd been certain she would never be happy again. No matter how bright and sunny the day outside, her world had been a dark place. She wouldn't consign her nephew to that kind of darkness. Losing an aunt he'd never met wouldn't hurt him; losing his mother would destroy something sweet and sacred inside of that little boy that would haunt him forever.

She held tight to Harley's hand, walking straight and tall as Adam led them into another room and abandoned them in the middle of a thick, padded rug that scratched the bottom of her feet. She didn't know if her father was watching, but if he were, she wouldn't show fear or give him any reason to doubt her when she told him to choose Harley.

"Welcome, ladies." Ian's voice oozed from somewhere in front of them. "I regret to have met you under such grim circumstances. Unfortunately, your father gave me no choice."

"I'm here, girls." Their father's voice sounded tinny and distant as if he were on speakerphone. It had been years since Hannah had heard his voice and even longer since she'd heard him sound so hopeless.

In fact, she'd only heard that particular sad resignation once before, on the day he sat her and Harley down to tell them that their mother had left the family. Maybe forever.

"Don't be afraid," Stewart continued. "I'm going to find a way to make this better. I promise, I won't—"

"Not this time," Ian cut in, a squeaking

sound following the words. It was the squeak of a chair giving under someone's weight, but Hannah couldn't tell if he was sitting down or standing up. "You'll honor your obligations this time, Mason. And to make it clear how very serious I am about the choice you're about to make…"

His words ended with a thunderous *boom! boom! boom!* that echoed off the walls, the gunshots deafening in the enclosed space.

Harley screamed and Hannah ripped the blindfold from her eyes, no longer caring about obeying the rules. If Ian had shot Harley, all bets were off. She would save her sister if she could and run if she couldn't.

Or maybe she'd hurl herself at Ian and see if she could claw his eyes out before he managed to kill her, too.

She spun, blinking at the sudden rush of light, to see that Harley had pulled her blindfold off, as well. Her sister's breath came fast and shallow as she backed away from the body beginning to bleed out at her feet.

Hannah swallowed, eyes flicking from Adam's paling face to the red stains spreading across his shirt. She fought to think past the horror clutching at her throat, struggling to figure out what this meant.

Ian had shot his accomplice. Adam was dead—or dying fast—and soon either she or Harley would follow.

Or maybe he'd shoot both of them, no matter what he'd told her father.

She hadn't had any experience in a hostage situation before, but her gut said that if Ian had his way, he would be the only one leaving this room alive.

CHAPTER TEN

Jackson

The moment Dom pulled the boat within five feet of the dock, Jackson jumped out and ran.

He wasn't worried about stealth or secrecy anymore. Gunshots had been fired. Three of them. Harley and Hannah could both be dead.

Or maybe Harley, Hannah, *and* Adam.

If Jackson knew his father, he wouldn't

allow a traitor to live. It didn't matter that Ian couldn't have taken Hannah without Adam's help or that his father had committed enough sins to thoroughly blacken his own soul. Ian had no tolerance for betrayal.

That was why Hannah was here. Her father had dared to betray a Hawke and now he was paying the price for it.

No, she's here because of you. You led Ian right to her.

If you hadn't been such a vengeful bastard, Hannah would still be safe on her island with her aunt.

Vengeful bastard. Just like his father.

As Jackson ran around the side of the house, bent double to stay out of sight of the ground floor windows, he cursed himself for growing up too much like Ian Hawke. If he hadn't been a madman bent on revenge, his father wouldn't have the woman he loved held at gunpoint right now.

He had to believe that Hannah was still alive. He couldn't admit that he was probably too late or he would start screaming and never stop. He couldn't lose her. Not now, not because he was five fucking minutes too late.

He was rounding the front of the house when he heard his father's voice and froze. He glanced over his shoulder, motioning for Dom—who was quickly gaining on his head start—to stay quiet before jabbing a finger at the open window above him.

"Now that you understand how serious I am, Stewart." Ian's voice sounded like he was facing away from him, but Jackson couldn't be sure. Slowly, he moved closer to the window, ears straining.

"You have two minutes to decide which of your daughters will live," Ian continued. "At the conclusion of one hundred and twenty seconds, I will make the choice for you."

Jackson's heart lurched into his throat. Hannah was still alive, but in less than two minutes she wouldn't be. There was no time for the diversion he and Dom had planned or to chart another course of action. He had to take advantage of the element of surprise and hope he could take his father down before he killed Hannah.

Pulling the gun from his pants, Jackson met

Dom's eyes and nodded toward the window. Without missing a beat, Dom motioned back around the house before drawing his own gun and hurrying back the way he'd come. Dom would cover the window on the other side of the room. If Jackson missed, hopefully, the other man wouldn't.

Slowly, Jackson stood up far enough to peer into the room, his stomach clenching when he saw Hannah and Harley on the other side of a large wooden desk. His father stood in front of the desk, his back turned to Jackson and his attention directed down at the open laptop beside him.

"Please, just give me a few more minutes." Stewart Mason's voice emerged from the computer. "I haven't spoken to either of the girls in years because of you, Ian. At least give me time to say goodbye."

"One hundred seconds," Ian said, proving his utter lack of compassion.

But then, he knew he was on a timetable and he wasn't one to waste time indulging other people's emotions. *His* emotions—his rage, his jealousy, his avarice—were all that mattered, all that had ever mattered.

Still, when Jackson stood up, aiming the gun at the back of his father's head, he couldn't help but hesitate for the barest second. He'd spent the past six years imagining the look on Ian's face when he realized that his son was innocent. He hated his father, but some part of him, that child buried deep inside of the hardened man he'd become, still craved his approval, his love.

But there was no love inside Ian Hawke. He was beyond redemption and it was past time for him to die.

Jackson was squeezing the trigger when his father suddenly turned and fired at the window, aiming right between his son's eyes.

CHAPTER ELEVEN

Hannah

It all happened so fast.

One second, her father was pleading for more time from the laptop screen; the next, Ian had turned and fired at the window behind him.

Hannah cringed, her shoulders hunching toward her ears as the glass shattered with another *boom! boom!* and a crystalline ringing that sliced through the air. Ian staggered backward, clutching his chest just as a third shot sounded from the other side of the room.

Acting on instinct, Hannah tackled Harley to the ground, rolling across the carpet as the window near the fireplace exploded.

"Run!" she shouted as they untangled themselves, urging Harley toward the entrance to the room. She had no idea who was shooting at the house, but they needed to get out of the room before they were caught in the crossfire. "Stay low, find somewhere to hide. I'm right behind you."

Harley scrambled out of the room on her hands and knees. Hannah was following when she caught a flash of movement out of the corner of her eye. It was Ian, lurching toward the window with his gun in hand, aiming at something outside. She came to her feet in the shelter of the doorway, standing on tiptoe until she could see the lawn outside and the wounded man sprawled on the grass.

She couldn't see his face, but she recognized the shape of Jackson's body instantly.

Her heartbeat stuttered and the blood in her veins turned molten as something primal inside of her responded to the sight of the blood staining his shirt with a roar of fear and rage. He'd been shot! His father had shot him in the chest. And now, unless she did something to stop him, Ian was about to finish the job of murdering his son.

The realization hit; a second later, Hannah was in motion.

She surged back into the room, her thoughts racing even as time seemed to slow, giving her a few precious seconds to think. As she rushed toward Ian, she snatched her discarded blindfold from the floor, wrapping it tight around her hands as she closed the last of the distance between them and leapt into the air.

She landed on the desk, skidding across the smooth surface on her knees to collide with Ian just as he lifted the gun and fired. His arm jerked down, sending the shot intended for Jackson burrowing into the baseboards. Before he could take aim again, Hannah wrapped the blindfold around his neck and pulled backward with all the strength in her body.

Ian thrashed and spun away, dragging her off the desk, but she held on, gritting her teeth and squeezing her hands into fists so tight her joints screamed in protest.

But she didn't let go. She clung to the fabric, using her body weight to her advantage. She let her knees go weak, sagging toward the ground, dragging Ian down with her. After a few more heavy steps, he bent backward, hanging halfway between the ceiling and the floor for a seemingly endless second before he collapsed on top of her, his torso pinning her hips and legs to the ground.

Panting for breath, Hannah kicked his bulk to one side and struggled free, her makeshift garrote at the ready and her eyes glued to Ian's face, which looked strangely peaceful now that he was unconscious.

The moment she knew Ian was out cold, the old Hannah would have jumped up and run to Jackson. But the new Hannah understood that you can't always run from your problems. Sometimes you have to fight for your life and the lives of the people you love. Now, that fighter inside of her insisted it would be dangerously stupid to leave this wounded predator alive. Ian would only wake up more determined to finish what he'd started.

As long as Ian Hawke was alive, none of the people she loved would be safe and she was tired of living in fear and being hunted for the sin of being Stewart Mason's daughter. Ian's revolver lay on the floor beside him, but she'd never shot a gun in her life and wasn't sure she could hold a weapon to a man's head and fire.

But she could finish this the way she'd started it.

Jaw clenched and a dark determination rising inside of her, Hannah straddled Ian's chest and brought the blindfold back to his throat. She was leaning forward, drawing the fabric tight across his windpipe when a hand touched her shoulder, making her spin and lash out.

By the time she recognized Dom's face, her

fist had already connected with his stomach, making him double over with a groan.

"I'm sorry," Hannah said, her voice soft and surprisingly steady. "I thought you were one of his people."

"I'm not," Dom said, grunting as he fought to catch his breath. "I'm on your side. Jackson's on the front lawn. He's been shot. It doesn't look fatal, but I need you to go apply pressure to the wound until your father's cleanup crew gets here."

Hannah glanced toward the laptop, but the computer was closed. The realization made her arms begin to shake. She hadn't even thought about her father or who else might be watching her murder a man.

Not that it would have changed her mind…

"Go check on Jackson," Hannah said, turning back to Ian. "I have to finish."

Dom's hand landed lightly on her shoulder again. "You already have, Hannah. He's not breathing, and I'm not going to administer CPR."

Hannah blinked down at the man beneath

her, unable to believe she'd been sitting on his chest for nearly a minute and hadn't realized that he wasn't drawing breath.

"Oh." She rolled off of Ian, her stiff fingers relaxing their grip on the blindfold as her hands began to shake.

He was dead. She'd killed a man. She was a murderer.

The knowledge should have done more than make her shake, but aside from her trembling hands she felt very calm, almost peaceful. She suspected she was going into shock, but she didn't have time to worry about it. She had to get to Jackson.

She stood, weaving slightly as the blood rushed into her legs.

"Are you okay?" Dom put a steadying hand to her back. "I can go to Jackson if you need a minute."

She shook her head, but before she could speak, a voice sounded from the foyer.

"Hannah! Hannah where are you?"

She turned to see Jackson round the corner and lean heavily against the doorway, clutching his right shoulder. He was grimacing and pale, with sweat beading on his forehead and blood streaming through his fingers to form tiny rivers that flowed down his left forearm, but he was alive.

He was alive and the most beautiful thing she'd ever seen.

She hurried to his side and tucked herself beneath his uninjured arm, gratitude rushing through her when he hugged her close with his usual strength. "You shouldn't be standing up."

"You're okay?" he asked, his pained gaze scanning her face. "He didn't hurt you?"

"I'm fine," she said, swallowing hard. "But your father's dead."

Jackson's eyes flicked to where his father lay on the hardwood floor, a small puddle of blood forming beneath his left shoulder.

"Your shot started it, but she finished it," Dom said, subtext in the words Hannah couldn't understand, but that Jackson seemed to.

"Good." He met the other man's gaze before turning back to her. "He would have killed both of us if you hadn't. Don't doubt it for a second. You only did what you had to do."

"We need to get the bleeding stopped," Hannah said, anxiety pricking at her skin as blood continued to seep from the wound near Jackson's shoulder, soaking his shirt. "Come on. Let's get you settled in the dining room."

"I'll find Harley," Dom said. "She has her pilot's license. She might be able to get us out of here before the cleanup crew."

"That would be great." The thought sent a wave of relief rushing through Hannah's chest. She wasn't surprised that Harley had acquired another exotic skill set. Her sister had always been a fan of acquiring new hobbies, especially ones that cost obscene amounts of money. "The sooner we can get Jackson to a doctor the better."

"We'll land at the airstrip near your father's house," Dom said, moving away down the hall as Hannah guided Jackson into the dining room. "He'll have a doctor waiting who won't ask questions."

Hannah's breath rushed out with a curse.

"Are you really okay?" Jackson asked softly.

"I'm understanding what a cleanup crew is correctly, right?" she asked, suddenly acutely aware of the acidic taste flooding her mouth. "People who clean up murder scenes so the bad guys don't get sent to jail?"

"Except this time they're cleaning up the murder scene so the good guys don't go to jail." Jackson grunted as he sat down on the edge of the heavy oak table and let Hannah help him lift his legs so he could lie down on top of it.

"Or the good woman, anyway," he added, paling as she wadded the blindfold into a ball and pressed it to his bullet wound. "You don't deserve to go to jail or even trial for this. It was self-defense."

"I wasn't thinking about myself," Hannah said. "When I saw you lying on the ground and your dad going in for the kill shot, I just…lost it." She shook her head, the dazed feeling still hanging around her head like a protective fog. She was grateful for the way it softened the edges of what she'd done, making it okay to push the sight of Ian's slack features from her mind. "I didn't even think about what I was going to do, I just did it."

"I understand. You were protecting what's yours."

Hannah held his gaze, her throat tightening as she searched his eyes for a sign that everything was going to be okay. "Are you? Still mine? Even though I ran away and nearly got us both killed?" She rushed on, cutting him off before he could speak. "I know you didn't give the order to kill Harley. I know it was a trick now, but I should have suspected that from the beginning."

Jackson's lips curved in a humorless smile. "It's not your fault. I didn't tell you that I'd put my people back on her trail. I should have." He paused, finding her hand with his. "The same way I should have told you that I love you long before last night."

"Yeah?" The lump in Hannah's throat swelled until she could barely breathe.

"Yes." Jackson squeezed her cold fingers. "I love you and it shouldn't have taken almost losing you to make me realize I never want to let you go."

Tears rose in her eyes and the numb feeling

began to fade, replaced by an overwhelming mixture of fear and relief that made her voice break as she asked, "Never?"

"Never," he said, without a hint of hesitation. "I'm yours. For as long as I'm on this earth. And I hope you'll be mine."

"Of course. Of course, I will." She smoothed his hair from his forehead before pressing a kiss to the sweat-damp skin. "I can't wait to be away from all this and know you're going to be okay."

"I'm going to be fine." He shifted, wincing as he moved his injured shoulder. "Don't worry. I've been in worse shape than this. Lots of times."

Hannah swallowed, willing her tears away, trying not to show how much the blood soaking the cloth scared her. "Well, hopefully, Dom will be back with Harley soon and we can get going." She nibbled her lip, dread knotting in her stomach as the reality that Jackson and Harley were about to set eyes on each other for the first time in years fully penetrated.

"I know you're still angry and you have

every right to be," she continued, "but I talked to Harley and I believe she's changed. That doesn't excuse what she did, not even a little bit, but I—"

"It doesn't matter," Jackson said with a small shake of his head. "I don't care about her. You're all that matters. You and me."

Hannah's mouth trembled, caught between a smile and something guiltier. "Well, anyway. I believe she's sorry at least. For what she did to you."

Because she had a child—maybe your child—and it changed her.

Love changed her, the way loving you has changed me.

She knew she had to say something to Jackson—warn him that Harley had a bombshell to drop—but she couldn't make her lips form the words. She told herself that she didn't want to upset him while he was wounded, but she sensed the truth was she didn't want to upset herself. After everything she'd been through in the past twelve hours, telling the man she loved that he could be the father of her sister's baby might be the straw that broke the camel's back.

Still, she was trying to put together a few coherent sentences, something she could say to ease tensions on the off chance that Harley brought up Jasper on the way to the plane, when Dom appeared in the doorway.

He was alone, a grim look in his eye Hannah didn't understand until she heard the faint drone of a plane engine flying low over the house, heading away to the east.

Her next breath emerged with a huff as she realized who must be flying the plane. "She left us. That's Harley, isn't it? Flying the plane? She left us here."

Dom dropped his gaze to the floor. "Looks like it. There's no one else on the property and I couldn't find her anywhere."

Hannah cursed, while Jackson laughed, a humorless sound that transformed to a groan. "Fuck, it hurts to laugh."

"Then don't," Hannah said, her voice sharp with rage. "There's nothing to laugh about. And if you die because she ran away and left us, I'm going to hunt her down and kill her myself."

Jackson tightened his grip on her hand. "No. No more hunting. No more revenge."

She glanced down at him, her anger fading a few degrees when she saw the love so clear in his eyes.

"We're going to get out of here," he continued, "I'm going to heal, and then you and I are going to make a life together away from all the crazy people in our lives."

"Yes," she whispered. "That's all I want."

Hannah leaned down to kiss his forehead again, silently willing the cleanup crew to move faster. The sooner she and Jackson were away from this place of fear and death and moving toward their brighter future, the better.

CHAPTER TWELVE

Jackson

Jackson did his best not to pass out, not wanting to scare Hannah, who he suspected wasn't holding up as well as she was pretending to for his sake.

But by the time the two burly members of Stewart Mason's cleanup crew arrived with a stretcher to carry him to the private jet, he was so lightheaded he couldn't fight the urge to sink into something deeper than sleep.

He blinked out and when he flickered on again—coming to staring at a vaulted ceiling in a room that smelled faintly of roses—he had no idea where he was, how he'd gotten there, or how much time had passed since he'd been shot.

Shot.

He'd been shot and his father was dead.

The memories came in a cold flood, making it hard to draw a deep breath.

He shifted on the crisp sheets beneath him, becoming aware of the IV in his arm—evidently the reason he wasn't desperately thirsty or suffering from more than a dull ache in his chest—and the woman asleep in the recliner in the corner. It was Hannah, in black spandex pants and a soft-looking red sweater, curled up with an afghan she'd wadded beneath her head to use as a pillow. Her hair was tangled, her face pale, and it looked like she might have been drooling on the blanket sometime during the night.

She was beautiful, so perfect and precious

his heart lurched, sending an ugly sensation coursing down his right arm.

He grunted softly as the pain came and went. As soon as the sound rumbled through his throat, Hannah bolted upright, blinking sleepy blue eyes in his direction.

"You're awake." She slipped out of her chair and crossed the room to his bedside, taking his hand as she perched carefully on the mattress beside him. "How do you feel?"

"All right," he said, his voice rough with disuse. "Pretty good really, considering. How long have I been out?"

"Almost two days," she said, worry clear in her eyes. "You lost a lot of blood. Thankfully, my mother was a match so the doctor was able to do a transfusion not long after we landed."

"I'll have to thank her." He glanced around the room, not sure how he felt about recovering in what he assumed was Stewart Mason's home. Stewart's money and connections had no doubt saved his life, but if Sybil's suspicions were correct, the man had also hired Ian to kill his own brothers.

"No, you won't," Hannah said, her tone brittle. "She wasn't happy about it. She wanted to let you die, but I convinced her to do it. For me."

His brows lifted and fell. "Well, I guess I'm lucky she loves you, then."

"I guess so." Hannah sighed, her gaze falling to their joined hands. "Or lucky she feels guilty or whatever it is that goes through her head when she looks at me."

She ran her free hand through her tangled hair. "I don't think it was really about you. Apparently, she had a thing with your father and it ended badly. She was never the same after the year she spent with him."

"What?" Jackson frowned. "You're kidding."

She laughed softly. "No, I'm not. That's why you became Harley's target. She wanted revenge against your father. So she decided to ruin his son in exchange for ruining our mother."

He relaxed back onto the pillows, strangely comforted by the revelation.

"You don't seem surprised," Hannah said,

peering at him through her lashes.

"I'm not. I mean, I'm surprised to hear about Ian's relationship with your mother, but I'm not surprised I was a target because of something he'd done. I'd thought of that before, that one of his enemies might have assumed the best way to ruin my father was to destroy his only child."

He glanced down at his wounded chest, his lips curving in a bitter smile. "Harley obviously didn't realize that Ian couldn't have cared less if I lived or died."

Hannah brought his hand to her lips and pressed a kiss to his knuckles. "I can't wait to get out of here." She glanced over her shoulder, before adding in a softer voice, "I don't trust Dad. He's been nothing but helpful and sorry, but it's clear he's not a fan of our relationship. And I can't shake the feeling that there's something he's not telling me."

"About what?" he asked, wondering if Hannah knew about Sybil's suspicions. He didn't imagine so, or she wouldn't be able to speak her father's name without horror in her voice.

She shook her head. "I don't know. I feel like it's something about your dad. Or your dad and my mom, something that happened while they were together maybe, but I know better than to push. If I do, he'll shut down and disappear and we'll be left alone with Mom and the maids."

"Might not be so bad," he said. "I'm not in any hurry to meet your father."

Hannah's lips pursed to one side. "Oh yeah? You're not planning to ask him for permission to court me?"

"I don't need his permission," Jackson said, holding her gaze. "I have your permission."

Her expression softened. "You most certainly do." She squeezed his hand. "Dom told me to tell you he's sorry for the things he said on the plane, by the way. He didn't give me specifics. He just said that you were right and I was stronger than he'd given me credit for."

Jackson grunted. "He should have apologized to you, not me."

"He did," she said, her smile fading. "And

then he left to go find Harley. She's given Dad's people the slip and disappeared."

"Why?" The mention of her sister's name sent nothing but a vague irritation flashing through his chest, proving that his lust for revenge was truly dead and buried. "My father's gone. The danger's over."

Hannah ducked her head. "Yeah, well, maybe she doesn't know that. Maybe she thinks he's still out there. Which means…"

"That she left without knowing you were safe," Jackson supplied with a sigh. "I'm sorry, Hannah."

She shrugged but didn't speak again for a long moment.

"Maybe it's for the best," he added gently. "I know you were happy to find out that she's alive, but she's not the kind of person you need in your life."

"I know I don't need her in yours," Hannah mumbled, keeping her gaze on the flowered quilt covering his legs.

"You don't have to worry about me." Jackson shifted his head, trying to catch her eye. "Look at me, Hannah." He waited until she reluctantly lifted her gaze. "I meant what I said. I'm not going to do anything to Harley. And I'm not going to go looking for her, either. Not anymore. I'm ready to let it go, to let go of everything except you and me."

"You promise?" Her eyes began to shine. "Even if you found out she'd done something else? You would still want to let it go?"

"Something like what?" he asked, brow furrowing.

She shook her head as she tilted her chin down, sending her tangled curls falling into her face. "Nothing. I don't know anything for sure. I didn't ask enough questions. I thought there would be time to talk later. But instead she ran away."

She laughed, a strained sound that ended in a soft sob. "I feel so stupid. I actually believed that she was sorry. I bought her lies all over again, the way I did when I was a kid."

Jackson studied her for a moment, unable to shake the feeling that there was something wrong.

Something more than you being unconscious for two days, her father being a criminal, her mother loathing her new lover, and her sister running off without bothering to make sure Hannah survived, you mean?

It was true. Hannah had been through hell and now wasn't the time to push her about Harley or anything else.

If he was going to prove to her that he was ready to let go of the past, actions would speak louder than words.

CHAPTER THIRTEEN

Jackson

"Can you get me a new cell phone?" Jackson asked, inspiration striking. "Something I can be sure my father's people didn't have traced?"

Hannah nodded. "Of course. I'll go to the store this afternoon."

"You should go now," he said, releasing her hand. "If I can reach the right people before noon, we should be able to fly out tonight."

Her eyes widened. "Fly where?" she asked eagerly, betraying her excitement before she shook her head. "No. You can't fly. You're hurt and you've been unconscious for two days."

"I'm fine to fly," he said. "But if you're worried I can make sure wherever we end up has a doctor on call."

She pegged him with a hard look. "A doctor who won't mind treating a gunshot wound without blabbing about it? I don't think so. We have to lie low, Jackson. My father said you're being investigated by the CIA."

Jackson snorted. "They've been investigating for years. If they haven't found enough to arrest me by now, they never will."

"Well, you'll forgive me if I'd rather we not put your hubris to the test." She closed her eyes and took a deep breath. "I just got you back. I don't want to lose you again to a prison sentence."

"You're not going to lose me," he said,

hating that he was the reason for the pinched, exhausted expression on her face. "I'm sorry."

Her eyes blinked open. "For what?"

"For coming to you with so much baggage," he said. "I'd undo it if I could, but I can't. All I can do is promise you that it ends here. From now on, I'll be conducting business strictly above board. Legal channels only."

Hannah smiled, a beautiful, hopeful smile that made Jackson swear he'd do whatever it took to keep it in place. "You don't know how happy I am to hear that."

"I do." He reached up to cup her cheek in his hand. "It's all over your face, sunshine."

She pressed her lips together. "For a while, I wasn't sure I'd hear you say that again. The past few days have been…pretty terrible."

"I'm sorry about that too," he said, scooting over to make room for her on the bed. "Come here, lie down with me."

"I'll hurt you," she said, but she was eyeing the empty space beneath his arm with a hunger that made it clear how badly she needed to be held.

"You will not." He clenched his jaw as he waved her onto the bed, refusing to show her how sore his other side still was. "And even if you do, you know I like a little pain."

She rolled her eyes. "Now's not the time for that."

"It's the perfect time," he said in a close approximation of his Dom voice. "So get your ass in this bed. Right now."

With a laugh, she climbed onto the bed and curled against his side, her head on his good arm and her palm resting lightly on his stomach. And even though it hurt, he hugged her closer. Pain and pleasure had always been tangled up with her, this woman he loved beyond all reason.

"I'll rest today, but tomorrow we're getting on a plane," he said, kissing the top of her head. "We'll find a peaceful place to celebrate the holiday and plan our next move."

"Our next move. I like the sound of that," she said with a wistful sigh. "Speaking of the holiday, I talked to Sybil yesterday. She and Hiro are back on the island. She said to give you her love and thanks when you woke up."

"I'm glad someone approves of our relationship."

"Yeah, that's nice, isn't it?" She sounded more amused than troubled by the fact that most of her family would be happier in a world without Jackson in it. "I told her it was all over and she was free to come home, but she's decided to stay. Hiro's going to help her fix up the bed and breakfast. Apparently he's moving in this week."

"You didn't tell her the truth?"

Hannah snuggled closer to his side. "No, I didn't. She's so happy and in love. And I figured that's Hiro's call. I believe he cares about her. If he's decided it's kinder to let the lie of why they met stand, I'm going to trust he has a good reason for it. I know honesty is important, but maybe sometimes it's kinder to give the person we love the gift of ignorance."

"Maybe you're right," he said, thinking about Sybil's suspicions about her brother, which she'd apparently kept from her niece for her entire life.

Maybe Sybil had come to the same conclusion that Hannah had, that sometimes it was kinder to keep the truth from the people we love. There was nothing to be gained from Hannah knowing that her father might have ordered the murder of his brothers. She obviously already knew that she couldn't trust the man. Learning that he was even more of a monster than she'd assumed would only hurt her and make her wonder how much of that DNA had made its way into her own genetic makeup.

Jackson knew what that felt like. He didn't know if he'd ever look in the mirror again without seeing the shadow of his father's sins written in the lines of his face. Hannah didn't deserve that baggage. She deserved happiness and peace and a life where the future was wide open.

Which compelled him to ask a question he wished he could avoid.

"What if I can't come all the way back, Hannah?" he asked, running his fingertips lightly up and down her arm.

She shifted, frowning up at him. "What do you mean? You're going to make a full recovery. The doctor said there wasn't any major damage."

"I don't mean that," he said, lifting his gaze to the ceiling. "I mean back from the things I've done. I'm not worried about a few days here and there, but I can't settle permanently in the States while I'm on a CIA watch list. And I don't know if that threat is ever going to go away. Your options will be limited because of me. After everything you've been through I wouldn't blame you if you needed some time to decide if that's what you really want."

Hannah propped herself up on one arm, bringing her face even with his before she said in a soft, but firm voice, "Don't even try it, Hawke."

He studied her, admiring the strength in her pretty eyes. "Try what?"

"To get away from me," she said seriously. "You're where I want to be. The rest of it is just geography."

An unexpected stinging sensation pricked at his eyes and his voice was hoarse when he said, "You're where I want to be, too."

Hannah's lips trembled into a smile. "Are

you going to cry?"

"No," he said, with a sniff. "My arm's hurting. That's all."

She made a cooing sound, kissing his cheek before she whispered against his skin, "You're the sweetest man in the world. Do you know that?"

Jackson grunted. "If you knew the dreams I was having about you while I was out you would know just how wrong you are."

"Oh yeah?" She pulled back, her eyes sparkling. "Were they dirty dreams?"

"Filthy." His cock stirred, the foolish thing too stupid to know he would hurt himself if he tried anything more than talk right now. "I had you tied up in a swing with your knees in your armpits and you were so fucking wet and begging me to take you. There were clamps on your nipples and—"

"Miss Hannah," a feminine voice called from out in the hall, making Hannah flinch, "are you ready for your breakfast tray, ma'am?"

"Leave it in the hall, please, Miriam," Hannah called out, holding Jackson's gaze as her hand slipped lower, sliding beneath the waistband of his pajama pants. "And bring another tray for Mr. Hawke, please. He's finally awake."

"Wide awake," Jackson whispered as Hannah gripped his erection and began to stroke him slowly up and down.

"Yes ma'am," Miriam said. "That's wonderful news."

"It is," Hannah agreed, tightening her grip until Jackson couldn't stop a groan from escaping his lips.

He lay back, focusing on keeping his heart from pounding through his chest as Hannah expertly worked his cock until he came so hard his vision blurred, smudging the sharp edges of the tray ceiling.

"Good?" she asked, kissing his throat, where his pulse still beat faster.

"Amazing," he murmured, running a palm over her hip. "My turn."

But before he could slip his hand down the front of her pants to return the favor, she'd squirmed away and slid off the edge of the bed.

"No, you're hurt," she said, reaching for tissues from a box beside the bed. "You need to rest and get your strength back."

"I don't need to rest." Jackson shifted higher on his pillows, ignoring the pain that flashed through his shoulder as he put weight on his injured side. "I need you to come on my hand."

She shot him a stern look. "No. You'll make your shoulder worse. I can tell you're in pain. I'll go call the doctor and ask if you can take something for it after breakfast."

"I'd rather have you for breakfast." He grudgingly took the tissues she offered, capturing her fingers and holding tight when she tried to pull away. "I could arrange to lie very still while you sat on my face."

Hannah rolled her eyes, a blush creeping up her neck. "You're impossible."

"I'm not impossible," he said, running a suggestive finger down the center of her palm. "You're irresistible."

"So it's my fault, is it?" she asked, letting him draw her closer to the bed.

Jackson nodded. "All your fault. Now get

back into this bed and let me finish what we started."

Hannah leaned toward him. For a moment, Jackson was certain he was going to have his way, but then another voice sounded from outside the door. This time, it was a man's voice, and there was little doubt in Jackson's mind who it belonged to.

"Hannah, I need to see you. It's urgent," Stewart Mason said, sounding much more self-assured than when he had been begging for more time to say goodbye to his daughters. "There's a letter here for you. I think we should open it together."

Hannah sighed, the happy light in her eyes flickering out as she called over her shoulder, "I'm coming. Just let me get Jackson settled with his breakfast tray."

"I'll meet you in the study." A moment later, Stewart's footsteps retreated down the hall.

"And a good morning to you too, sir." Jackson's lips curved in a rueful smile. "He seems excited to hear that I'm awake."

Hannah grimaced. "I'm sorry."

"It's not your fault," Jackson said. "None of this is your fault."

"I know, but I wish things were different. I kept hoping…" Hannah trailed off with a shrug. "I don't know. I guess all the time apart tricked me into thinking my parents were better people than they really are."

"Absence makes the heart grow fonder."

"Absence makes the heart grow stupid," she said, tossing the tissues into a small trashcan near the bedside table.

"You're not stupid," he said in a firmer tone. "I don't want to hear you talk about yourself that way."

Hannah looked up, a smile curving her lips. "Yes, sir."

"Go see what he wants," Jackson said gruffly, shocked to find himself stirring again, simply from hearing those two words tumble from her lips. "And then bring me a secure phone so I can start plotting our path to freedom."

"Yes, sir," she said again, with a little salute.

Jackson growled. "Don't tease me, sunshine. Or you'll be sorry. I'm not going to be a gimp forever."

She winked. "I'm terrified, sir. Truly."

He couldn't help but smile. Smile and tell her again, that he loved her.

"I love you, too," she said, her playful mood vanishing as she crossed to the door, opening it to reveal an older woman in a simple gray sweater and khakis holding a breakfast tray.

"Perfect timing, Miriam." Hannah scanned the plates and bowls artfully arranged on the tray. "And you made sure these are from the list of foods approved by the doctor?"

"Yes, ma'am." Miriam nodded. "Mr. Hawke can start with broth and if that settles well, I've got oatmeal and toast with honey."

"Wonderful, thank you so much, Miriam." Hannah turned over her shoulder, shooting him a tight smile as she stood back to make way for the maid to enter the room. "I'll be back to check on you soon."

Jackson nodded. "All right." He resisted the urge to tell her to hurry back, instead focusing his attention on Miriam, thanking her for the tray she settled gently across his lap.

He was already an invalid. He wasn't going to start acting like one of those needy bastards who couldn't stand to be separated from his other half for more than ten minutes at a time. And he wasn't going to let himself get sucked into creating problems where none existed.

Everything was fine. Hannah was safe, the danger to her life had been eliminated, and they had agreed to share their life together for the foreseeable future. All they had to do was get out of this house and away from her parents and things would go back to normal.

As normal as they ever had been, anyway. But he wasn't going to let that bother him, either.

He and Hannah might not be normal, but they could and *would* be happy together. He refused to contemplate the thought of anything else.

CHAPTER FOURTEEN

Hannah

Hannah took the envelope from her father, frowning at the broken seal. "I thought we were going to open it together."

"I couldn't wait. I was too worried." Stewart leaned in, templing his fingers as he watched her pull the letter from the envelope. "And it seems I was right to be. It's from your sister."

Hannah glanced up at him, fighting a wave of irritation. "Are you going to let me read it, Dad? Or should I just ask you what it says?"

Stewart's brows crept higher on his broad forehead.

"I apologize," he said in a tone that made it clear he thought he had nothing to apologize for.

"As I said, I was worried." He motioned toward the letter. "Please. Read. I'll wait until you're done and we can discuss it together."

She took a deep breath as she turned her attention back to the letter, determined not to let her emotions show on her face as she read.

No matter how much she wanted to believe the danger had passed and she was finally safe to relax her guard and reestablish a relationship with her father, she couldn't shake the "off" feeling that made her nerve endings itch whenever she was in Stewart's presence.

Her gut said that her father still had secrets, dangerous secrets that might threaten the peaceful future she yearned for.

Dearest, sweetest, bravest Hannah,

Hannah resisted the urge to sneer at the effusive address.

It seems I'll never come to the end of asking your forgiveness, but I do hope you'll forgive me for leaving without saying goodbye.

I waited to make sure you were okay, but then I had to leave. It was my one chance to get away and get to Jasper before Dad's people figured out where he was. We worked out a special hiding place years ago and I knew he would be there, waiting for me, and we would finally have the chance to start a life away from all the sins and miseries of the past.

Some of those sins are mine, but most of them are Dad's.

I'll leave it up to him how much he wants to tell you. I would tell you everything, but I know it would cause you pain.

And I'm sure Dad will intercept this letter before you're allowed to read it—Hello, Dad, and goodbye, you sick son of a bitch—and my truth-telling would do no good. He would destroy the letter without passing it on and I would never get to tell you how much I love you.

And I do love you, so very, very much.

You are still my Jiminy Cricket, moo.

You're my conscience and the voice that leads me to all the best and brightest places. It's your voice I've listened to for the past six years as I've fought to be the kind of mother Jasper deserves. And it is because of Jasper—and the Hannah voice in my head that insists his welfare must come first, no matter what—that I have to disappear again. He deserves to grow up happy and safe, with none of the ugly past shadowing his future.

I hope there will come a day when it's safe for us to be a family again, but until then, know that I am out there somewhere in the big wide world loving you with all my heart and wishing you happiness.

If you've found that with Jackson, then I wish you both well.

But don't let him make you pay for the things I've done, moo. You are your own person and a better one than I could ever be. The similarities between us are only skin deep, as you know better than anyone.

Take care and may the years ahead of you be happy ones, my sister friend.

Never ever,
Harley

Hannah pressed her lips together, fighting to regain control of her emotions.

The letter left her torn between being touched and suspicious, hurt and saddened that she'd lost Harley all over again.

But more powerful than any of those feelings was the certainty that her father was hiding something. Something bad, that Harley had known would cause Hannah pain. Something that had made her sister call the father she'd once idolized a "sick son of a bitch."

Once upon a time, Hannah would have talked around that line.

But when she looked up to find Stewart's face set in his usual "master of all he surveys" mask, she couldn't think of a valid reason to let him off easy.

"What did you do?" She set the letter on the table beside her wingback chair, suddenly cold despite the fire roaring in the fireplace near her feet.

Stewart sighed wearily as he pinched the bridge of his nose between two long, thin fingers. "Aside from do everything in my power to protect you and your sister? And nearly have a heart attack when I thought I was going to lose one of you?"

"Yes," Hannah said, not buying the worried father act for a moment. "Aside from all that."

He glanced up, studying her with his shrewd blue eyes. "I did what had to be done. It wasn't gentle, but it was necessary. Your sister discovered a small part of an ugly, old story and rushed to judgment. If she'd given me the chance to explain, she would have understood that I did the best that I could. Considering the circumstances."

Hannah didn't bother trying to pick that tangle of words apart. She simply squeezed her lids closed, her features scrunching into a tight wad at the center of her face.

"There are things you don't understand, Hannah." Her father sighed again, a more put upon sound this time. "Will you stop making faces and look at me, please?"

She opened her eyes, pinning him with a cool glare. "Are you going to tell me what those things are? Are you going to explain what you did to make Ian Hawke your enemy? Or what Harley found out that made her think the only way to keep her son safe was to run away and hide in a place where you could never find her or Jasper?"

He sat up straighter, a new stiffness creeping in to tighten his jaw.

"That's what I thought," Hannah said, rising from her chair. "Jackson and I are leaving tomorrow, Dad. If you change your mind and want to be honest with me, then I'd love to have an adult conversation about this. If not, don't bother contacting me again. And don't send any spies or people to protect me. I don't want or need your kind of help."

Stewart made a grumbling sound. "You absolutely do need protection. As far as most people are concerned, you're the last living daughter of one of the richest men in the world. That will make you a target, Hannah. Ian wasn't the only person after my money or willing to hurt my children in order to—"

"You don't have children anymore, Dad." She ignored the pained look that flashed behind his eyes.

"You have me," she continued. "For now. But if you insist on lying to me, you will lose me too. I can forgive a lot, but I can't forgive being kept in the dark about things that could endanger my life and my family."

"*I'm* your family." Stewart stood, spreading his arms in a gesture that insisted he had nothing to hide.

A gesture that was just another lie.

"Jackson is my family," she said firmly, needing him to understand that she wasn't making idle threats. "I'm going to build a life with him and I hope someday we'll have children. Children I will love and do everything in my power to keep safe because nothing will be more important to me than their health and happiness."

"That's what I've done, Hannah. God, can't you see—"

"No, Dad, that's not what you've done," Hannah said, refusing to back down. "If my safety were truly your first priority, you would tell me the truth. I need the truth. I can't protect myself from something I don't understand."

"You don't need to understand, you need to trust your father."

Hannah's breath rushed out in an exasperated huff. "Maybe when I was a child, Dad, but I'm not a child anymore. I'm a grown woman, who has lost years of her life hiding away from the world, all to help you protect your secrets. Because your secrets are the most important things in your life, not me or Harley or Mom or anyone else."

Stewart balked but didn't say anything for a long moment, long enough for Hannah to notice how gray his hair had become and the way his eyes sagged at the edges.

Her father didn't have smile lines. He had creases in his stony face, marks caused by gravity, not by the soul contained within his body.

Suddenly, that seemed like the saddest thing in the world, to have lived over sixty years and bear so few signs of a life filled with love or laughter.

Finally, he spoke, his voice rougher than it had been before. "I'm leaving you everything, Hannah. The fortune, the estate, the businesses, everything. You can look at my will if you don't believe me. I have a copy in the desk drawer."

It wasn't what she'd been expecting to hear, but it wasn't what she needed to hear either. "I don't care, Dad," she said, fighting to keep her frustration from her voice. "I don't care about the money. I never have, don't you know that by now?"

"I've been in touch with Sybil. I know your business is in trouble." Stewart folded his arms, scowling down his nose at her in that way that used to make her shake in her shoes when she was a girl. "I could make your problems go away. Or I could cut you off without a penny, and let you see how hard the world can be without money to smooth your way."

Hannah stood up straighter, meeting his scowl with a hard look of her own. She wasn't a little girl anymore, and she wasn't the fragile, bendable daughter her father had known, either.

"Go right ahead, Dad," she said, feeling like she'd shrugged off a lead weight from around her shoulders. "I'm capable of making my own money. I'm also capable of surrounding myself with people who understand the difference between love and manipulation."

She turned to go, but her father called out for her to wait. She turned back, eyebrows raised, waiting for him to give her a reason to stay.

"I…I don't know what to do," Stewart said, his arms falling limply to his sides. "I don't want to lose you. I just…I don't know how to make you stay."

Her chest flooded with a tender, wounded feeling, pity and anger swirling inside of her until finally both emotions faded away, leaving her as confused as the tired old man facing her across the room.

"I'm not a chess piece, Dad," she said wearily. "I'm your daughter. I'm a person and I'm willing to listen if you're willing to talk."

He blinked, his features softening in a way

she had never seen before.

But it wasn't regret or love that gentled his expression; it was hopelessness, helplessness, the barren look of a man who had finally realized that the war was over and he had lost the final battle.

No matter how much he might want her to stay, he couldn't, or wouldn't, let her in. He was trapped inside a fortress of his own lies and he would remain there—safe, but desperately alone—until the day he died.

"I did what I had to do," he said in a voice not much louder than a whisper. "There's no point in talking about the past. It's too late for regret. Or forgiveness. You couldn't forgive it all, anyway. No one could."

Hannah nodded, tears stinging into her eyes as Stewart settled back into his chair by the fire, clearly resigned to letting his daughter walk away.

To the outside world, her father appeared to have it all—money, power, influence, a beautiful, well-bred wife, and a shot at the presidency if he played his cards right. But looking at him now, all Hannah saw was the shell of a man, a lonely, suffering warning that every dream came at a price.

The price her father had paid had been too dear, and it had left him all alone.

He would rule his kingdom from a dusty, empty tower room, knowing that everything beautiful in his life had withered and died in the shadow of the dark bargains he had made.

Tears slipping silently down her cheeks, Hannah turned to go, wondering how high a price she would pay for her own dreams.

She waited until she was down the hall, nearing the garage on the south side where the servants parked before she pulled her cell from the band of her sports bra, where she'd had it tucked since last night. Dominic said he would call as soon as he had news, but she couldn't resist punching in his contact number and hitting send.

The phone rang four times before forwarding to voice mail.

For a moment, Hannah considered hanging up without leaving a message, but if she was in for a penny, she was in for a pound.

It was time for Dom to know just how

serious she was about getting the information she needed.

"It's Hannah," she said after the beep. "I took some samples of Jackson's hair last night while he was sleeping. I'm overnighting them to the post office box address you left so you'll have them as soon as you're ready. Hopefully, finding Harley and Jasper won't be as difficult as my father seems to think it will be and we can have this settled soon."

Hannah hesitated a moment before adding. "And Dom, don't forward any information to my father. I know we agreed that you work for me now, but I want to make it clear that I don't want Dad to know where Harley and Jasper are. She had her reasons for wanting out from under his thumb and I respect them, whatever they are. Talk soon."

She hung up and stood in the dim light at the end of the hallway, squeezing the phone tight, wondering when she had become the kind of person who has spies on retainer.

Or the kind who collects hairs from the pillow of her unconscious lover, proving she was as concerned about her own peace of mind as she was his precious life.

She didn't know, but she knew she couldn't back down now. She had to know the truth. Then she would decide how much to tell Jackson and whether or not she could live with keeping his son a secret from him for the rest of their lives.

LILI VALENTE

CHAPTER FIFTEEN

Jackson

They landed in Jackson Hole, Wyoming four days before Christmas and barely made it to their cabin on Granite Ridge before the snow began to fall. By midnight, the gentle drifting flakes had become a madly swirling blizzard and Hannah spent half the night crawling in and out of bed, making sure the power hadn't gone out and taken the heat with it.

No matter how many times Jackson assured her that he was firmly on the mend, he knew she was concerned about the isolated state of the cabin and worried about what would happen if his health took a turn for the worse. He also knew that he should be grateful for her love and concern, instead of frustrated by the constant reminder of his own vulnerability, but he couldn't help wishing she would stop worrying.

He was just so damned grateful to have her back and safe. He wanted to enjoy loving her and let things between them go back to normal.

But worry seemed to be Hannah's new default setting and things remained far from normal. She still refused to do anything but sleep in their shared bed, insisting she was too afraid of hurting him to make love gently, let alone anything else. Jackson intimated that there were games they could play that had nothing to do with rough stuff, but Hannah acted as if he'd suggested she punch him in his bullet wound so he'd let the matter drop.

They had time. There was no need to rush

or push Hannah to drop her guard before she was ready.

They spent the next three days reading by the fire and watching the snow cover the valley below their window, but the energy between them wasn't the same as it had been on the island. Before, they'd enjoyed easy silences. Now, something lived in the air between them, an unspoken fear Hannah refused to name. Every time he asked her what was bothering her, she would smile and insist that everything would be better as soon as she knew he was really going to be okay.

He wanted to believe her, but couldn't shake the feeling that something had changed, something that might not be as easily mended as his flesh and bone.

By the time the snow melted enough for them to drive into town for supplies on Christmas Eve day, Jackson was going stir crazy and desperate for a chance to prove to Hannah how rapidly his health was improving. They had breakfast at the Four Seasons and then drove to the town square.

There, the fresh snowfall made the Old

West style buildings look like something out of an antique Christmas card and strings of brightly colored lights lit up the archway of elk antlers marking the gateway to downtown. Jackson had never been a fan of the holidays—any holiday—but as he and Hannah stepped out into the brisk morning air, he found himself looking forward to exploring and picking out a few surprises for Christmas morning.

"So where do we want to go first?" Hannah asked, looping her arm through his and huddling close to his side though he knew it was more to offer him support than to absorb his warmth. In her heavy white wool coat and white rabbit skin hat, she was more appropriately dressed for the weather than he was in his thick black sweater. "The art gallery looks interesting."

"It does," Jackson agreed as he gently detangled her arm from his. "But *we* aren't going anywhere. *I'm* going to need a little time alone to buy presents."

Hannah scrunched her nose, but he could see the smile she was trying to hide. "You don't have to get me anything."

"I know I don't have to," he said. "I want to. Let's meet at the Cowboy Bar in an hour. We can have another coffee and check out the gallery after."

"An hour," she repeated, nibbling on her bottom lip.

"Do you need more time?"

"No, I don't need more time." She reached up, adjusting the tension on his sling for the third time this morning. "I'm just worried about leaving you alone for an hour. You only have one arm."

"One arm is sufficient to get my wallet out of my pocket and put it back in again," he said dryly. "I don't plan on buying any souvenir antlers so I'll be fine to carry the packages, too."

Her frown remained in place. "But what if you get tired? Or what if something happens and you need my help?"

"Nothing's going to happen." Jackson forced himself to smile. "I'm fine. The pain is manageable, the wound is closing well, and I haven't had any fever in five days. It's time to relax."

"But you've been resting for the past five days," she said. "You haven't been traipsing around all over the place shopping and exhausting yourself in the dead of winter wearing nothing but a sweater."

"The sling wouldn't fit with my coat and I'm not going to be traipsing, I'm going to be walking at a sedate pace."

"But—"

"I've never traipsed a day in my life," he pushed on. "I wouldn't know how to traipse if I tried and shopping is hardly in the same league with the amount of exercise I'm used to doing on a daily basis."

"You don't usually have a bullet hole in your chest on a daily basis," Hannah grumbled, but he could tell that she'd realized it was time to cut the apron strings. Or at least let them out a little.

Thank God. As sweet as her concern was, he was starting to feel suffocated.

"Fine, go shop," she said with a sigh. "But call me if you get too tired or need my help. And make sure you're at the Cowboy Bar in exactly an hour or I'm going to come looking for you. And I'm not going to be happy when I find you."

You aren't happy now. The thought flashed through his head unbidden, leaving him feeling the cold for the first time this morning.

She *wasn't* happy and he couldn't help feeling like it was something more than his injury causing the sparkle in her eyes to dim.

As he kissed her goodbye and crossed the street, bound for a local crafters' store and the jewelry store beyond, he decided it was time to put an end to the weird dynamic between them before things got any worse. And he suddenly had a good idea how to start bringing them back together.

Hannah was a strong woman who had proven how brave she was, but she was also submissive. *His* submissive.

She'd given him so much trust in such a relatively short amount of time. She'd abandoned herself to him, trusting in his strength and control, and then he'd been shot, proving that he was flesh and blood like any other man.

"No wonder she's scared," he mumbled as he pushed into the crafters' store and was enveloped in a rush of warm, dry air, feeling like an idiot for not sensing the reason for her withdrawal sooner.

But Domination wasn't only, or even primarily, about flesh and blood. Domination was about power exchange and trust as much as sex toys and spankings. He might not be able to throw Hannah over his shoulder and tie her up in a sex swing anytime soon, but he could still take her to the place of safety and abandon she had come to crave. He could still make it clear that he was in control and she could trust him with her pleasure and her pain.

But you can't promise not to die, leaving her vulnerable and alone.

Jackson frowned down at a row of antler bracelets and delicate white bone earrings carved into lace displayed in the case in front of him.

"Can I get something out for you?"

He glanced up to see an older woman with

gently weathered brown skin and bright green eyes watching him from the other side of the display, her long graying hair pulled into a bun and her trim form encased in various shades of brown fleece. There was nothing remarkable about her—aside from the pretty shade of her eyes—but Jackson was struck by how relaxed and happy and *normal* she seemed.

This was the kind of life Hannah would have had if he hadn't taken her away from her aunt or taught her to crave sharp edges and pain with her pleasure. When she was happy, it was easy to defend the love they'd found, but watching her fret herself into losing five pounds in four days made him wonder if he was doing the right thing.

No matter how much he loved her, would his love be enough to keep her happy in a world designed for people like this? Normal people who didn't get off on games played in the shadows?

"Maybe these aren't quite your speed," the woman continued, seemingly unfazed by Jackson's lack of response. "That's all right.

Bones and horns aren't for everyone."

"No." He shook his head. "I mean yes, you have some very nice things. I'd like to see the earrings, please. The ones on the far left."

With a smile that crinkled the edges of her eyes, the woman unlocked the case and reached inside. "Excellent choice. These are my absolute favorites. It's amazing how Becky can make a little piece of animal bone look like a scrap of lace like that."

Jackson picked up one of the earrings, letting it dangle from his thick fingers, feeling clumsy and out of place. It had been so long since he'd bought a woman a gift, and even longer since he'd wanted her to like it as much as he wanted Hannah to like the things she unwrapped tomorrow morning.

He only wanted to please her, but somewhere between losing her in Tahiti and finding her in Florida with her hands creased and red from the fabric she'd used to kill a man, he seemed to have lost the knack for it.

"It's delicate but still strong," the woman mused, studying the earring from the other side of the case. "A beautiful contrast."

Delicate, but strong. Like Hannah.

"I'll take them," he said, setting the earring back beside its mate. "Do you gift wrap?"

"Not usually." The woman's grin widened. "But seeing as you're in a bit of a bind with that arm and it's the day before Christmas I can make an exception. Just let me go beg some paper from my friend across the way. Be back in two shakes of a lamb's tail."

Jackson nodded, moving off to one side of the case as two teenage girls pressed up against it, studying the bracelets.

It was true, bones and horns weren't for everyone. Neither was the lifestyle he and Hannah had chosen, but they could make it work, as long as he remembered to take care of every part of her—the strong and the delicate, the tender lover and the stubborn worrier who drove him crazy, the brave defender of the people she loved and the frightened woman who looked at him like he might vanish before her eyes leaving her alone.

But he was made of tougher stuff than that and as soon as he got Hannah home he was going to prove it.

With that in mind, he decided against the charm bracelet he'd been planning to buy her at the jewelry store, opting instead to look for something with a more significant meaning.

CHAPTER SIXTEEN

Hannah

Hannah barely had time to hang her hat on one of the many hooks inside the door and unzip her coat when Jackson slammed the door behind them and ordered—

"Clothes off, on your knees by the fireplace."

Startled by the abrupt return of his Dom voice, she spun over her shoulder, arousal and unease flooding through in equal measure, leaving her feeling like a light socket that had started to short circuit. "B-but you're still in pain, I don't think—"

"I didn't ask what you thought. I told you to take your clothes off and get on your knees." He tossed the bag he'd brought in from the car onto the floor and prowled toward her, a hungry look in his hooded eyes that made it clear he meant business.

Or pleasure, rather.

This was the side of Jackson that she usually associated with pleasure, the side that could make her knees weak with a look and her panties damp with a single command. But right now she didn't want to play games. She was too worried—about him, about the future, and about what Dominic was going to find out now that he'd tracked Harley and Jasper to a village in southern Thailand.

Just the thought of her secret calls to her new spy was enough to cool her desire.

"No. I don't want to, Jackson," she said, hanging her coat beside her hat.

Before she had time to say another word,

he was across the wide foyer, his good hand fisting in her hair.

She gasped as his fingers tightened at the nape of her neck, her bones melting the way they always did when he touched her like this—like she was his to pleasure or punish as he saw fit. She hadn't realized how much she missed the thrill of danger mixed with seduction until he drew her tight to his chest and spoke in a dark whisper—

"You don't tell me no. No is not in your vocabulary when I want you naked and kneeling. Do you understand?"

Hannah bit her lip, torn between the lust spreading, hot and thick, through her mid-section and the fear that Jackson was going to hurt himself trying to prove something that didn't need to be proven. She was his. She belonged to him and they belonged together and there would be time for the game when he wasn't barely a week into healing from a gunshot wound.

"No is in my vocabulary when you're being an idiot," she said, arousal mixing with the anger in her tone. "I'll get on my knees, but you have to promise to sit down and take it easy."

"You don't give orders," he said, using the fist in her hair to half drag her across the room to the fireplace, proving he had more strength left in that big body of his than she'd assumed. "You don't tell me when to sit still or shut up or stop asking for what I need from you."

"Jackson stop, I—" Her words ended in a cry of pain as she tried to pull away and he answered her attempt by tightening his grip at the base of her neck.

"I'm hurt, but I'm not dying and I've still got more than enough mental and physical strength left to top you, sunshine." His voice was so deep she could feel it vibrate the tips of her nerve endings, sending a fresh sizzle of desire tingling across her skin, making her nipples pucker. "Now take your clothes off and get on your knees. This is your last chance to have this end well for you."

Hannah glared up at him, her breath coming harsh and uneven. She was turned on, there was no doubt about it—and it was clear he was determined to have his way, even if he ended up ripping his stitches in the process— but instead of reaching for her sweater zipper, she shouted the first word that came to her mind.

"No!" Her volume was loud enough to echo through the room, but saying it once wasn't enough. Now that she'd started, she couldn't seem to stop. "No, no, no!"

"No?" Jackson repeated, soft and cold, his control stoking her anger.

"No!" she howled, barely resisting the urge to punch him in the stomach. "I said no, damn you, so let me go!"

"No isn't the word you use," he said, again in that completely calm, even tone that made her want to scream. "If you want this to stop you use your safe word. Anything else I'm going to assume is a challenge to up my game until you feel safe again."

"I'll never feel safe," she said, tears spilling down her cheeks, shocking her. She hadn't even realized she was about to cry.

"And why's that?" He pulled her closer, pinning her to the strong side of his body though she squirmed to get free. "Why can't you feel safe?"

"I don't know," she sobbed, overwhelmed by terror and rage she hadn't known she was feeling. "Let me go. I don't want to touch you right now."

"Why? Am I hurting you?"

"No," she snapped, then added with a sob, "Yes, now let me go."

"I'm never going to let you go," he said, vulnerability flickering behind his eyes. "You're mine. Your pleasure and pain are mine, your happiness and sadness are mine, your fear and hurt are mine." He leaned down, pressing his lips to her forehead before adding softly, "But I can't help you control any of those things unless you give me the reins, Hannah."

She sucked in a breath, fighting to keep her face from crumpling. "But I'm afraid," she said, trembling as the truth she'd been hiding from herself came clawing its way to the surface.

"What are you afraid of?" he asked, his voice gentle now though he didn't loosen his grip on her hair.

"You said you had respect for life, but not hers," Hannah said, a dam breaking inside of her. "You said you would never doom your child to having her for a mother. But what if you did, by accident? What are you going to do?"

Jackson froze before pulling back to look down into her face.

"What are you going to do?" Hannah choked out between sobs as Jackson's hand slid from her hair. "You can't take her son away. She loves him more than anything. I don't know what else to believe about Harley, but I believe that. Jasper is the only thing that matters to her, the only thing she's living for."

His lids closed, concealing his eyes, so she had no idea what he was thinking.

"I wanted to tell you right away," she babbled on, her nose beginning to run. "But I didn't have a chance to find out if Jasper was yours and I didn't want to upset you while you were trying to get better." She sucked in a breath. "But most of all I didn't want to think about you having a baby with my s-sister. I hated the thought so much I wasn't sure I was going to tell you, even when I knew the truth for sure."

She sniffed hard, ashamed of herself now that her secret was out. "But I should have been honest with you, even if I didn't want to be. I'm sorry."

Jackson's eyes opened, but he didn't look at her. He kept his gaze on the ground as he nodded toward the fireplace, "Sit down on the couch. I'm going to bring you something to drink."

Hannah gulped. "But I don't—"

"Sit down, Hannah," Jackson said, loud enough to make her jump before she backed away to sit down hard on the supple leather couch cushion.

She threaded her fingers together in her lap, heart racing as she watched Jackson move across the large open room to the kitchen. The average person wouldn't be able to tell that anything was wrong, but Hannah could read the tension in his movements as he fetched a glass from the cupboard and filled it with water from the refrigerator door.

He was upset, most likely angry, too, but her mind couldn't think past the relief coursing through her.

No matter how much she dreaded the conversation they were about to have, she was so grateful to sense the miserable distance between them beginning to fade away.

She accepted the glass Jackson offered and took a long drink as he crossed the room to the bookshelf and plucked a box of tissues from beside a set of leather-bound classics. By the time he returned—placing the tissues within her easy reach before sitting down on the wooden coffee table facing her—she'd stopped crying and was ready to accept whatever came next.

Even if he yelled at her or shut down and pushed her away as punishment, it would be better than the disconnect of the past week.

"Tell me everything," he said, the muscle leaping in his jaw the only outward sign of the stress he must be feeling. "Don't leave anything out, even if it seems like something small."

Hannah set her water on the side table near

the lamp and took a bracing breath. "Harley and I were locked in a room at your father's house. She thought she was going to die, so she asked me to promise to take care of Jasper, her son, and love him like he was my own. I didn't find out much about him except that he's five and getting ready to go into kindergarten this coming year."

Jackson nodded, but his expression remained emotionless. "So the timeline is right for him to be mine. But I know she was sleeping with at least one other person that summer."

"Right," Hannah agreed, her stomach cramping. "Your friend. And there could have been others. Harley wasn't a big fan of monogamy back then." She tucked her thumbs inside her rolled fingers, resisting the urge to nibble the rough edge of her cuticle the way she did when she was nervous as a child. "I should have asked her who the father was, but I was too busy trying to figure out a way to get out before Adam or Ian came back."

"As you should have been," Jackson said.

"Your safety is the most important thing."

Hannah dropped her gaze to the dark jewel tones of the carpet. "But if I'd asked, then I wouldn't have hired Dominic to spy for me or stolen your hair from your pillow while you slept."

Jackson sighed. "For a DNA test I assume?"

Hannah kept her eyes focused on the floor. "Dominic found Harley and Jasper yesterday. They're in Thailand. He's hoping to have samples of Jasper's hair soon and the test results not long after."

"And you've been worried that I would try to take the boy away from Harley. If it turns out he's mine."

"Not consciously," she said, shoulders hunching. "I didn't realize I was worried about that until it just…came out."

He grunted softly. "And I thought you were pushing me away because you'd put so much trust in me and I'd betrayed it by going and getting myself shot."

Hannah glanced up sharply. "No, I... It has nothing to do with that, Jackson."

"Are you sure?" he asked, searching her face. "I imagine it would be scary to submit to someone and then have them prove they're not as strong as you thought they were."

"You were shot. That has nothing to do with strength or a lack of it," she said, wanting to reach out to him, but sensing he wasn't ready to be touched. "And I didn't mean to push you away. I just couldn't be the way we are together and keep a secret from you at the same time."

"No, you can't," he said. "I can't either. Trust is important in any relationship, but for us it's going to be critical. This is only going to work if we're honest with each other. Even when it hurts."

She nodded, pressing her lips together and fighting the tears trying to rise in her eyes. "I know. And I'm sorry."

"It's all right. I'm not in a place to judge," he said, running his good hand through his hair, which looked even silkier and shinier away from the island humidity. "I've been keeping something from you, too. Something your aunt told me when she learned you'd been taken."

Hannah sat motionless as Jackson briefly outlined Sybil's suspicions, absorbing the news that her father might have hired Ian to kill his brothers with less shock than she would have expected. But then, she'd sensed he'd done something horrible, something so dark and terrible that he would never be able to find the other side of it.

"I didn't want you to have to live with that," Jackson continued. "I didn't want you to wonder if there was some part of you—no matter how small—that was like him."

Hannah blinked, shocked by the ping of recognition deep inside of her. "I probably wouldn't have thought of that, at least not at first. But you're right. I will wonder. I guess a part of me already has been."

She bit her lip as she shook her head slowly back and forth. "I've changed so much in the past few months, but it hasn't really felt like change. It's felt like the real me, the person I kept hidden for so long, finally stepped out into the light and sometimes…" Hannah hesitated, but then forced herself to push on, knowing if anyone would understand her fears it would be Jackson. "Sometimes that person scares me."

He reached out, taking her hand. Energy hummed from his body to hers, filling her with the certainty that she wasn't alone.

"She shouldn't scare you," he said. "I love her. Even when she makes mistakes."

Hannah's mouth trembled. "But I killed a man. And I didn't...I *don't* feel bad about it. I really don't."

"*We* killed a man," he corrected. "And you shouldn't feel bad about it. It had to be done. There's a reason my mother hasn't reported him missing or called the authorities, Hannah. My father was a monster who had nothing left to offer the world but more violence and suffering." He squeezed her hand. "Regretting ending his life is a waste of energy you could be using to not keep secrets from me."

Her lips quirked at the edges before settling back into an uncertain line. "What are you going to do? About Jasper?"

"I don't know," he said with an openness that surprised her. "I'll wait until we know if the boy is mine and if he is… We'll decide what to do then."

"We?" she asked, brows lifting. "So you're not angry with me?"

"No," he said, before adding in a drier tone, "I'd prefer nothing like this happens again, but I'm just glad to get to the bottom of it. I've hated the distance the past few days. You've felt…out of reach, and I didn't like it."

"Me either." Hannah slid to her knees in front of him, bringing her palms to rest lightly on his thighs. "If you still want me naked and kneeling, I'm ready."

He cupped her cheek. "To be honest, I'd rather make love than play. It seems like that's the side of us that needs attention right now." He grimaced lightly. "And though I hate to admit that you're right, after dragging you around my chest hurts like hell."

"Well, you were right, too." She turned her head, pressing a kiss to his palm. "I needed you to push me. If I hadn't needed it, I would have said my safe word." She curled her fingers into the thick muscles of his thighs, skin prickling as his fingertips traced a trail down her throat. "But that scares me sometimes, too. The way you seem to know me better than I know myself."

"I don't. I've just had more experience with power exchange."

"It's not just that." She dropped her head back, staring up into his beautiful face as he clasped the zipper holding her sweater closed and dragged it slowly down. "When my head feels clear, I love the game. I crave it and don't feel like I've gotten close enough to you if we go without it for too long," she said, voice breathy from a combination of longing and the prickle of fear inspired by being so vulnerable, even with someone she knew she could trust with her most breakable parts.

"But when you bring out things in me that I didn't even know were there," she continued, "it can start to feel like I'm out of control in a bad way. Does that make sense?"

"It does." He pushed her sweater off one shoulder and then the other.

Hannah caught her sleeves with opposite fingers, tugging the cozy knit down until it fell to the floor, leaving her in nothing but her camisole. Immediately, her nipples puckered, the combination of the cool air in the cabin and Jackson's fingertip slipping beneath one strap enough to make her nerve endings spark violently to life.

"But that just means we've reached territory we haven't explored before," Jackson continued, finger teasing up and down the length of her strap without easing it off her shoulder. "It's unfamiliar, but it doesn't have to be scary."

"But what if we reach ugly territory?" she asked softly. "Or territory you just don't care for?"

"I care for everything about you." His hand stilled as he held her gaze. "I care for the little girl you were, the woman you are, and the person you're going to become. When I said forever, I meant it. I don't make those kinds of promises lightly."

His warm fingers slipped down the front of her shirt, capturing her nipple and rolling it gently, but his eyes remained glued to hers, heightening the intimacy of the electric touch. "Tonight I'm going to prove that by making love to you until you understand that there is nothing I want more in the world than to be close to you. And tomorrow, I'll prove it by showing you that I can handle anything and everything you need to give me. How does that sound?"

"It sounds perfect." Hannah swallowed, fighting back another wave of tears. But they were grateful tears this time, the tears of a woman who was loved exactly the way she needed to be loved—sweet and gentle, hard and ruthless, coaxing and demanding, and everything in between.

"Now take off the rest of your clothes," he said, leaning in to kiss her forehead, his breath warm on her skin. "It feels like forever since I've seen you."

Knees already weaker, Hannah stood, studying Jackson's face as she unbuttoned her jeans and pushed them down to the floor. Her socks came next, then her camisole, and finally her panties. She hooked her thumbs at the sides of the lacy fabric, drawing them slowly down her hips and thighs until she reached the place where a gentle shimmy of her legs sent them slipping down her calves to fall at her feet.

The entire time, Jackson watched her, his eyes filling with a mixture of hunger and tenderness that made her feel like the most beautiful woman in the world. By the time she finished her brief striptease, she was wet and aching, so eager to be joined with him that she hoped he wouldn't delay their gratification for too long.

There were times when she craved teasing and a slow spiral out of control. But there were times when she simply needed to be as close as she could get to the man she loved, this dangerous man whose arms had become the only place where she felt safe.

Once, not long ago, she had been afraid of what Jackson would do next. Now, the only thing she feared was that, for some reason, she might not be around to see it.

Or that someone would take him away from her before she had time to love him in all the ways—and for all the years—she wanted to love him.

CHAPTER SEVENTEEN

Jackson

Jackson's breath caught and his fingers flexed restlessly at his sides, torn between reaching for Hannah and taking another moment to drink in how beautiful she looked.

"Maybe you were right about the other, too." Her tongue slipped out to dampen her lips as he did his best to memorize the way her skin glowed in the cool winter light filling the room. "Looking at a man like you, the last thing I used to think about was death. But now, I do. I think about death, and how quickly it can take away everything that matters."

"I think about that, too." Jackson stood, encircling her waist with his good arm, ignoring the dull pain throbbing through his bum shoulder as he hugged her close. "I thought about it the entire flight across the ocean to Florida, hating myself for failing to keep you safe and worrying that I'd waited too long to tell you the way I feel."

He leaned down, inhaling the smoke and winter smells lingering in her hair, an ache filling his chest that had nothing to do with his gunshot wound. But it was a sweet discomfort, the increasingly familiar pain of his heart stretching wider, making room to love her more.

"I promised myself if I got a second chance, I wouldn't hold anything back," he continued, hugging her closer, wishing he could draw her so close that nothing—not even death—could ever pull them apart. "I can't say with any certainty what happens after this life, but if energy can neither be created nor destroyed, neither can love like this."

She tipped her head back, tears filling her eyes even as she smiled that wide, nothing-to-hide smile he'd missed so much. "I would never have imagined the first law of thermodynamics could be so romantic."

"It isn't romantic; it's the truth," he said, hand slipping down to mold to the bare curve of her bottom. "Some part of me has always loved you. And some part of me, the best part, always will."

Hannah blinked fast, her throat working as she reached up to take his face in her hands. "What did I do to deserve you?"

His lips curved in a wry smile. "Nothing. Or everything, depending on which me we're talking about."

"There's only one you," she said with a confidence that made him believe he would continue to put the darkest hours of his life behind him. "And I love him and I need to take his clothes off as soon as possible."

His smiled widened. "Immediately works

for me."

Hannah reached for the strap on his sling as he thumbed open the close of his jeans. A few moments later, she was back in his arms, her skin cool against the burning length of his cock as they backed toward the couch. She arched her hips as they moved, rubbing against his erection, making him groan as his lips found hers and his tongue pushed inside.

He needed to be inside her so desperately his balls felt bruised and tender, but he needed to kiss her everywhere first. He needed to claim her mouth, taste the honey and musk of the skin beneath her breasts, plunge his tongue into the slickness between her legs until he could feel her pussy pulsing around him, flooding his mouth with evidence of her desire. He needed to make love to the backs of her knees and the small of her back and the place at the base of her neck that made her melt when he trapped it between his teeth and bit down.

"Sit," Hannah murmured against his lips as the back of his knees hit the couch. "Let me do the work so you don't have to put weight on your arm."

"This isn't work. This is all I've been able to think about lying next to you every night," Jackson said, but he allowed his weight to settle back onto the cool leather cushions, the thought of watching Hannah ride him too tempting to resist.

His cock jerked as she straddled him and his tip began to leak, but when she reached down to guide him inside her, he gripped her wrist and pushed her hand away.

"Not yet," he said, cupping her breasts in his hands. "I need to kiss you here first."

"Be careful," she said, breath catching as his thumbs brushed across her tight nipples. "The doctor said you shouldn't use that arm except when you're working on the physical therapy exercises."

"This is physical therapy." He drew his tongue across her nipple, moaning as the singular taste of her skin filled his mouth.

"Seriously, Jackson, I don't—" Her words became a gasp as he sucked her deeper, trapping her taut flesh between his teeth before flicking his tongue back and forth until she squirmed on his lap.

"Oh, God. God, Jackson." She threaded her fingers into his hair, holding on tight as he tortured her sensitive skin. "I've missed you. So much."

He transferred his attention to her other breast, shifting his leg until it was wedged between her thighs. Her hips undulated as she rubbed against him, riding his leg until her slickness coated his skin and his balls began to pulse with a heartbeat of their own.

Her breath grew faster and more erratic, her arms trembling as her fingernails dug into the skin at the back of his neck, sending a hot knife of pain through his pleasure, giving him the strength to draw out the anticipation for a little longer.

"Now your mouth," he said, continuing to tease her slick nipples with his fingers as he tilted his head back. "Give me your mouth."

Hannah leaned in, her lips parted as if she knew he meant to do something much more thorough than simply kiss her. And he did. He was going to show her who her mouth belonged to.

Her lips, her teeth, her tongue—they were all his. Every inch of her was his and he meant to make sure she knew it.

He drove his tongue into her warm, wet heat, fucking her mouth with the thick muscle, plunging in deep and hard until she had no choice but to relax her throat and open for him. She groaned, the sound vibrating their lips as he stroked deeper, his tongue dancing with hers as his grip pulsed on her nipples, pinching her skin between his fingers a little harder each time, until she was bucking into his leg.

Finally, she ripped her mouth from his with a gasp. "I'm going to come, Jackson. I can't stop it, I can't."

"Wait," he ordered, gritting his jaw as he reached down, squeezing her hip tight with one hand while he positioned his cock with the other. "Wait until I'm inside you."

"Yes, please." She bit her lip, whimpering as he guided his engorged head back and forth through her slick, swollen folds, unable to resist a few more seconds of sweet torture. "Please, Jackson. Please!"

"Not yet, wait for me," he said, circling her clit with his leaking tip though his balls were suffering and he wanted to be inside her more than he'd ever wanted anything.

But he wanted them both even closer to losing control, so close that the razor edge of their desire would cut away everything that stood between them. "Wait, Hannah. Wait for me."

She made a sound that was half growl and half plea for mercy but held still, waiting for him to give her permission to move.

"Look at me," he said, needing to look into her eyes as she tumbled over. "Now, sweetness. Ride me now."

With a sob of relief, Hannah spread her thighs and dropped her hips, taking him deep, deep, deeper, until he was clutched in her heat, feeling her inner muscles squeeze tight around him.

But she didn't come. She bit her lip and held his gaze as she bent her knees and hooked her feet around the inside of his knees, giving her more control over the length and duration of her thrusts as she began to slide up and down him, fucking him with a slow, languid rhythm that scattered the coals threatening to burst into flames within him.

Jackson brought his hands to her sides, letting them skim the surface of her silken skin as she moved, so lost in her eyes he couldn't think what else to do with them. They'd made love like this before—close and connected, with her gaze locked on his, telling him so much more than words ever could—but this time it was even more intimate, more intense. He was naked with her in a way that had nothing to do with their physical bodies and everything to do with trust and love and the indestructible energy they created together, something so pure and right Jackson wouldn't have believed it existed before her.

Before Hannah, his love, his light, his everything.

"Everything," she echoed as if he'd said the words out loud.

But he supposed he had. There were ways to speak without saying a word. Her touch, her kiss, the shine in her eyes as she began to move faster, carrying them both closer to the precipice, told him as much as her words. They said he was loved and seen and exactly what she needed, no matter what the rest of the world might have to say about it.

"Closer," he said, bringing his hand to the small of her back. "I want to feel your skin against me."

She leaned forward, breasts rubbing against his chest as her hips pumped harder, faster. He shifted closer to the edge of the cushion, giving himself more freedom to move, to thrust up into her as her rhythm grew frantic and her breath came in shallow gasps that puffed against his lips.

"Are you going to come for me?" he asked, loving the sob that hitched her chest as she nodded. "Then come, baby. Come on my cock, let me feel you."

The skin around her eyes tightened as her pussy locked around him, but they didn't close. She kept her eyes open, staring into his as they came together, riding the sharp edge of their pleasure until it became a gentler wave, carrying them home even as it eroded more of the shoreline that separated them.

Someday soon, there would be no separation at all, nothing to keep him from the kind of union he hadn't known he craved until Hannah had proven to him that love was more powerful than anything that stood in its way.

"I love you," she murmured long minutes later, her lips kissing his throat as she spoke.

Even in the middle of claiming her pleasure, she had been careful to collapse on his uninjured side, but Jackson wasn't sure it mattered. He was suddenly feeling better than he had since the day he was shot, the bliss of union and release making him wonder if they needed to wait until tomorrow to attend to their other needs.

"And I'm so hungry I feel like I could eat all of the groceries we left out in the trunk," she said, her stomach confirming her claim with a long, irritable growl that made Jackson smile.

"Then why don't you go grab them," he said, patting her ass. "And I'll make you something decadent for lunch."

"You?" She lifted her head, shooting him

an incredulous grin. "You're going to cook for me?"

"I'm an excellent cook," he said with a sniff that she apparently found funny.

She giggled, forcing his softening length from inside her, sending a ripple of regret skimming through him and making him even more determined to have her again before the day was over. He hadn't had his fill of her yet, not nearly, but he could wait long enough to prove that he had skill sets beyond those he'd proven in the bedroom.

"Get the bags, woman." He delivered a more serious swat to her backside, loving that it only made her smile wider. "I'm going to make you a lunch that will make your mouth come."

Hannah's eyes darkened. "Is that right?" Her tongue swept out, teasing across her lips. "Is that even possible?"

"Haven't you learned not to doubt me, yet," Jackson said, his blood beginning to simmer all over again. "I don't make promises I can't keep."

She sobered, a tender expression softening

her face. "No, you don't. It's one of the many things I love about you." She kissed his cheek before slipping off his lap. "Let me get a cloth from the bathroom to clean up and I'll get dressed and get the bags."

"You don't have to get dressed," he said, admiring the sway of her hips as she crossed the room to the hall leading to the downstairs bathroom. "There's no one close enough to see you run outside."

"I'm not going out in twenty-degree weather naked, Jackson," she called out. "I enjoy a little pain, not torture."

He smiled. "But you'd look sexy wearing nothing but those furry boots you bought today."

Her laughter echoed down the hall as she came back into the room carrying a damp rag in one hand, a dry one in the other. "We can live out that fantasy later. Indoors."

Oh yes, they would. They would live out that fantasy and more.

Now that they'd reconnected and put the strangeness between them aside, it was time to make sure their other needs were met. There would be time to wonder what the hell he was going to do if he had a son he'd never met later. There would be time to sort out where he and Hannah went from here and what to do with his life now that he'd left his criminal past behind him.

But the rest of the day was his and Hannah's, and he intended to make sure it was a Christmas Eve neither of them would ever forget.

CHAPTER EIGHTEEN

Hannah

Jackson couldn't chop vegetables one-handed, but he was excellent at telling her how to slice them to his satisfaction—big surprise. She teased him about being a control freak in the kitchen as well as the bedroom, but he only smiled and said—

"I want the carrots thinner, sunshine. I know you can get them thinner than that."

—and returned to whipping up an exotic blend of spices and cornmeal that he said was going to transform his version of chicken and dumplings into something taste-bud-orgasmic.

Hannah kept sneaking glances his way as they worked, surprised by how sexy she found it to see him moving confidently about the kitchen, setting water to boil and the oven to preheat. But she shouldn't be, she supposed. Everything about him was sexy, from the way he fisted his hand in her hair and pushed her out of her comfort zone to the way he held her gaze as she rode him, the look in his eyes making it clear there was nothing in the world that mattered to him as much as her happiness.

Whatever came next, they would face it together and they would come out whole on the other side. She believed that now. She'd made a stupid mistake, but instead of lashing out or getting angry, he'd simply forgiven her. As much as anything he'd said or done in the past that easy forgiveness made her certain she'd found the only person she wanted to share her life with.

It also made her wish he could see himself through her eyes. He shouldn't worry about what he might have inherited from his father. Jackson was one of the best people she'd ever met, a fact he proved as he cooked her an amazing lunch, helped clean up one-handed, and tucked her in for a nap though she could tell he was interested in more entertaining bedroom activities.

But she was exhausted from the stress of the past week and the adventures of the morning and determined to keep him from putting any more weight on his wounded side until tomorrow morning.

Besides, it was the perfect afternoon for a nap.

Outside the floor to ceiling picture windows of their loft bedroom, a gentle snow had begun to fall, coating the mountains with another layer of white, blurring the edges of the world until it felt like everything outside of their warm cocoon of covers was distant and small. Everything that mattered was right here, lying beside her with his fingers running lightly up and down her back as she snuggled close to his chest and fell into the deepest, most peaceful sleep she'd enjoyed in days.

She slept hard, soaking in much-needed rest, and woke slowly, drifting back into her body with the nagging feeling that something wasn't quite right. Her skin was still warm from the flannel sheets and her head cradled by her pillow, but when she opened her eyes, the world remained dark.

She blinked, her lashes brushing against whatever it was that covered her eyes. She moved to pull the fabric away, but when she tried to shift her arms, she realized what else had changed since she'd fallen asleep. Her wrists were bound together and tied above her head and the bra and panties she'd worn to bed were gone.

She was naked, blindfolded, and tied to the headboard.

She was also immediately, mind-numbingly aroused.

Her lips parted to call out to Jackson and let him know she was awake, but before she could speak, a large hand covered her mouth and a rough voice whispered in her ear.

"Relax, sunshine, it's just me."

They were the first words he'd ever spoken to her, all those years ago when he'd made love to the wrong sister and proven there was nothing more right than the way they fit together. And now, they were going to relive that first time, knowing exactly who they were making love to.

Hannah moaned against his hand, wanting to tell him how perfect this was, but he kept his hand firmly over her lips.

"Remember when I told you I'd do all the dirty things you wanted me to do, as long as you would say you were mine?"

She nodded slowly, all of her available senses on high alert, not wanting to miss a moment of what he had planned.

"Well, now you're mine," he said. "Are you ready to play?"

"Yes," she whispered, lips moving against the rough skin of his palm.

"Good," he said, in his deep, delicious Dom voice. "But from here on out, don't speak unless you need to say your safe word."

She nodded again and his hand vanished, the mattress dipping as it gave up his weight. She wet her lips and rubbed them together, finding it harder to stay quiet than she usually did. The fact that she couldn't see what he was doing made her crave other forms of communication, but she forced herself to remain silent, listening to him move around the room.

She heard a rough scraping sound followed by a sizzle and a whiff of sulfur that made her think he'd lit the candle on the bedside table. A moment later she heard his footsteps at the bottom of the bed, but then nothing. She held as still as she could, straining for some sign of what he was up to, her nerves growing progressively agitated as more time passed and nothing happened.

He didn't touch her, he didn't talk to her, he didn't give any sign that he was even still in the room, let alone in the midst of an erotic encounter.

Seconds became minutes and minutes seemed to drag on for hours as she lay tied to the bed, the sheets growing damp beneath her as she began to sweat. The air in the room was cool, but not knowing what the hell was going on was driving her crazy, ratcheting up her body temperature until she felt like she'd just come in from an afternoon on the slopes.

Finally, when her arm started to itch in a place she couldn't scratch, the soft sheets began to feel rough and gritty against her sensitized skin, and frustration had tied her throat into knots, she let her breath huff sharply through her lips.

She had no idea what Jackson thought he was doing, but she didn't like this game, not one bit. "Jackson, where are you?" she asked, her irritation clear in her tone.

In less than a second, he answered her.

Hannah cried out as his hand curved around her hip, flipping her roughly onto her stomach. She barely had time to lift her face from the pillow when his hand came down hard on her ass. She cried out, back arching as he delivered another stinging swat to her other cheek, alternating back and forth until her flesh began to burn.

CHAPTER NINETEEN

Hands balling into fists, she fought to keep still and not to cry out—in pain or arousal—sensing her punishment for breaking her silence would be worse if she did. The spanking continued for twenty strokes and then thirty as Hannah's teeth dug into her lip. Her bottom flesh flamed so hot she was sure her ass must be bright red, and her pussy grew slick and swollen, jealous of so much attention being paid to another part of her body.

By the time Jackson finished, she was breathless from a heady combination of pain, arousal, and uncertainty about what he was going to do next. They'd never played a game like this before and the newness of it was nearly as nerve-racking as it was arousing. Nearly…

Fortunately, this time she didn't have long to wait.

"Trust means believing that I'm always there for you," he said in a soft, controlled voice. "Even when you can't see me. Even when your head tells you that my focus is elsewhere."

His fingertips traced the valley of her spine, collecting the drops of moisture that had gathered there as he spanked her. "But I am always thinking of you, always focused on you. There is nothing that matters to me as much as you and your trust and obedience when I'm proving that you're mine. Nod if you understand."

Hannah nodded, her head buzzing drunkenly as he gently urged her over to lie on her back. She was already high on the scene and they'd barely gotten started. She had a feeling Jackson didn't mean this encounter to be a mild one, and that she should do her best to hold onto her sanity as long as possible, but she didn't want to stay sane.

She wanted to get lost in him, in the things he did to her. She wanted to fall and fall and know that he would always be there to catch her.

"I'm going to tie floss to your nipples," Jackson said, his finger circling one tip and then the other, making her breath come faster as pleasure shivered from her breasts down to the hot, needy place between her legs. "I'm going to tie it tight enough to hurt, but not for your skin to go numb. If the pain is too much, use your safe word. If not, keep silent. Now arch your back."

Hannah obeyed, arching into his fingers as he plucked and teased her nipples into tight points and then wrapped each one in a little knot of torture. But it was delicious torture, the kind that made her nerve endings sizzle and her sex even wetter.

She held still for as long as she could but finally couldn't resist the urge to shift her thighs, restlessly seeking to ease the tension fisting between her legs.

"It looks like you're ready for more," Jackson said, a hint of amusement in his tone. "Spread your legs as wide as you can, sunshine. We're going to see how you like pain in a more intimate place."

Hannah slowly drew her legs apart, pulse leaping in her throat as she wondered what he was going to do next. Would he tie floss around her down there? And if so, how exactly would that work?

She was nibbling on her bottom lip, torn between eagerness and trepidation, when Jackson ran a finger down the center of her, making her entire body jerk in response.

"You're so wet," he said, his voice husky. "So responsive. I love seeing how much you want me."

His finger moved to one side of her entrance, pinching one of her outer lips lightly between his fingers before something harder pinched more firmly just below it. "I'll start with one clothespin on each side and give you a minute to adjust before I add more."

Pressing her lips together to suppress a whimper, Hannah held still as he applied a pin to her other side.

Dreamily, she swam through waves of hot and cold, exploring the pain and pleasure drifting through her as, after a moment, Jackson applied the next set of clothespins. He waited a long, sizzling moment before bringing a finger to her clit and tapping gently.

"This is not to make you come," he said, slowly, torturously tapping, hard enough to make her aware of how desperately she wanted release, but not enough pressure to take the edge off. "This is to remind you that even when I'm causing you pain, your pleasure is always utmost in my mind. I know you don't like one without the other, but there are times when you need this more than you think you do. You need to be reminded why you gave me your trust in the first place."

A second finger—or maybe a thumb, she couldn't be sure—found the tight puckered muscle of her ass and began to exert a similar pleasure.

"And I need your submission just as much. Nothing makes me feel safer or more loved than to know you trust me enough to give yourself to me. Completely." His thumb tested her hole, offering just enough pressure to make her aware of how much she wanted him there, too.

She wanted him in her ass and her pussy. She wanted him so far down her throat she couldn't breathe. She wanted him to fill her up, everywhere, in every way, because he was so exactly what she needed.

He was everything she wanted before she knew she wanted it. He was the mystery she would spend the rest of her life unraveling and never solve because he wasn't that kind of man. He wasn't a man you pinned down and sorted out; he was a wide, endless wilderness she could explore forever. He was the person she would keep falling deeper and deeper in love with until the last day she shared with this man—her lover, her master, her friend.

"I love it when you obey me without

question," he said, words thick with desire. "But I love it when you make me work for it, too. Because every time you push me, I'm going to push right back."

He emphasized the words by slipping his thumb into her ass, drawing a soundless gasp of relief from her throat. It wasn't his cock or even close to everything she wanted, but it was a small mercy, a little more of him, the one thing she needed above all else.

"And every time we push," he continued, beginning to fuck her ass with slow, shallow strokes, driving her arousal even higher, "I see parts of you I've never seen before. And the more I see, the more I love you."

Hannah spread her legs wider, relishing in how right it felt to be pushed to the edge of what her body and soul could take. Yes, she wanted pleasure, but she wanted this, too. She wanted deeper and closer. She wanted to be seen and loved in ways she hadn't known were possible until she'd become Jackson's.

"But I see more of myself, too," he said, gently withdrawing his hand from between her legs. "While I was watching you sleep, I kept thinking about the ways people try to become the best versions of themselves."

The mattress dipped and she felt his heat beside her. "Some people use religion." He pressed a kiss to the side of her breast, bringing her attention back to the stinging pleasure of her bound nipple. "Some use a shrink or art or exercise or self-help books."

He flicked his tongue across her aching tip, summoning a sigh of bliss and surrender from her lips. "We use each other. And for everything I learn about being a better, stronger man, I'm rewarded by getting a little closer to you."

She swallowed, overwhelmed with sensation and emotion and not sure how much longer she could resist the urge to speak.

"So never doubt that you can trust me, sunshine," he said, urging her onto her side with a firm hand. "I won't hurt you, I won't let you down, and I won't leave, no matter how deep we go or what we find there." He curled his body behind hers, his cock teasing at her entrance, making her want to sob with relief. "I couldn't escape from you any more than I could escape from my own skin, and I wouldn't want to."

The erotic torment had driven her to the edge, but it was the love in his voice as he proved that he understood her better than anyone in the world that made her break.

She pulled in a breath, not sure what she was going to say, only that she had to say something, when he whispered against her neck—

"Tell me if this makes the pain too intense."

—and pushed inside her, his thick cock spearing through where she was so swollen and wet.

She cried out, a desperate, guttural sound that came from a primal place inside of her only Jackson had ever reached. His thrust stretched the sensitive skin where the clothespins gripped her, intensifying the sting until it hurt, but the hurt was soon eclipsed by the bliss of Jackson sliding home, filling her completely.

Her head fell back with a groan. "Yes, sir."

"Yes, it's too much?" he asked, breath hot on her neck.

"No, sir," she panted. "Not too much. I like it. I love it. I love you."

"I love you, too." He kissed her shoulder, a tender kiss that became something darker when he parted his teeth and bit down, summoning another groan from her throat and a rush of heat between her legs.

"Yes, yes," she chanted, arching her back, easing the way for his next thrust to shove a little deeper. "Don't stop, sir. Don't ever stop."

With a growl, Jackson wrapped his arm more tightly around her waist, holding her tight as he began to fuck her harder, faster, driving them both toward that bright, clear place at the end of the game where they would burn together.

Hannah's fingers clawed at the air above her head and her arm muscles pulled whip tight, desperate to touch, to hold, to reach back and dig her fingernails into the thick muscles of Jackson's ass as he rode her, but she was bound too tight to escape.

And damn if the frustration didn't drive her need even higher.

By the time Jackson's palm slid down her belly to her clit, she was already a whisper away. All it took was the barest pressure of his fingertips on her sensitized skin and his sharp command to, "Come for me," and she was gone.

Gone. Lost. Found. Above it all but more a part of Jackson than she had ever been before.

Even as pleasure turned her body inside out, drowning her in bliss and magic, she was still with Jackson, so in tune with his every movement, his every breath, that she knew the exact moment he joined her in the fall. His cock swelled thicker, hotter inside of her and he came in long, wrenching bursts that made him cry out in what sounded like pain.

But it wasn't pain that made him squeeze her tight, holding on for dear life as they rode the waves of pleasure together. It wasn't pain that made him mumble sweet, wonderful things she could barely understand in her ear as they writhed together, drawing out the release until it felt like they would be like this forever, tangled and twisted and lost together in the best way.

And it wasn't pain that made him kiss her cheek tenderly as he removed the pins, the binding on her nipples, and the soft fabric tying her hands before reaching for the back of her blindfold and slipping the knot free.

Hannah blinked as she rubbed feeling back into her hands, waiting for the fuzziness to fade from the edges of her vision before she turned to look over her shoulder to find Jackson propped up on his good arm watching her. "Hi," she said, feeling shy, the way she sometimes did when they went somewhere new together.

"Hi," he said, lips curving in a soft smile.

Hannah was returning the grin when she saw the blood staining the bandage covering Jackson's bullet wound and concern swept in to banish the rosy post-scene haze. "Jackson, you're bleeding."

"I don't care. It was worth it," he said, still smiling as he caught her arm, holding her on the bed beside him when she would have jumped up to grab the first aid supplies. "Stay. It won't hurt to put off a new bandage for ten minutes."

Hannah sighed as she relaxed back onto the sheets, knowing that yelling at him wouldn't do any good now. And at least it wasn't a lot of blood.

Besides, she didn't want to leap out of bed just yet. She needed a few minutes to stare up into his eyes while her head and heart absorbed all the things she'd learned. "You're really good at that," she finally said.

"At what?" His smile went cocky around the edges.

Hannah laughed. "All that. All that *that* that you did just then."

"I'm glad," he said, grin fading though his eyes still sparkled. "I meant it. You make me better. This makes me better."

"I know. Me too." She turned, curling closer to his chest, inhaling the sweat and sex smell of him, knowing it would always be one of her favorite scents in the world. "I don't think we'll ever reach the end of that road, do you?"

"No." He rested his hand on her ass, giving her an affectionate pat. "But it sure will be fun trying."

She giggled again, so sated and pleasured and content that she was certain she wanted for nothing. And then Jackson said—

"Will you marry me, sunshine?"

—and she realized that there is always room for a little more happiness.

She propped up on one arm, meeting his soft gaze, awed that this was the same man she'd met two months ago. He was still strong, stubborn, and determined to have his way, but now he was also thoughtful and caring and loved her with a bravery that was humbling.

"Should I wait and ask again tomorrow morning?" His eyes searched hers, the spark of uncertainty in their depths as sweet as it was unnecessary. "I had something romantic planned involving mimosas, but I just…I didn't want to wait."

"Me either," she whispered, leaning in to kiss him with her next words. "Yes, Jackson Hawke, I will marry you."

"Thank you," he said, the relief in his voice making her smile against his lips.

"I'm already yours. Might as well make it official."

He hummed appreciatively into her mouth and kissed her gently, but thoroughly.

And as they made love again—slower and sweeter this time, coming together with the unpracticed ease of two people who were made to fit just right—Hannah silently gave thanks for the man in her arms. He was precious, irreplaceable, and no longer anything close to a monster.

He was all man now.

And all hers.

LILI VALENTE

EPILOGUE

Two months later
Jackson

They were married in Samoa and decided to stay. Tropical islands without extradition treaties weren't easy to come by and the fact that Samoa was relatively close to Tahiti and Hannah's aunt was all it took to seal the deal. They settled into a cottage by the beach, spent their honeymoon making love until they lost track of where one of them ended and the other began, and started shopping for investment property.

After years of running an apparently cursed bed and breakfast, Hannah was reluctant to get back in the lodging business and Jackson had no interest in opening a restaurant or tourist shop. His finances were in excellent shape, but he preferred to operate businesses that were easier to keep in the black.

Near the end of January, Hannah had found a job working for a charity that helped native women start small businesses that lifted their families out of poverty. While Jackson was proud of her and the good work she was doing, he missed their long days on the beach and became increasingly aware that he had gone soft during his recovery.

He stepped up his workouts and eventually fell in with three men who ran the same route he did every morning. Over post-run coffee at a local café, he learned that they owned a gym near the town center and worked part time providing security for visiting dignitaries. Once they heard about Jackson's service in the marines, they were eager to hire him on to the team.

Needing something to occupy his hours while Hannah was gone, he agreed, with the stipulation that he had to be home no later than six Monday through Thursday and he never worked Friday through Sunday, Hannah's days off.

And so it was that Jackson found himself wearing a gun holster and an ear piece, standing outside the Chinese embassy in Apia, waiting for the ambassador he was shadowing to conclude his business for the day when a man in a straw hat and a white guayabera shirt walked out of the covered market across the street and up the steps into the shade beside him.

Normally, Jackson would have immediately been on alert, but there was something familiar about the man, something that put him at ease, even when the stranger stepped a little too close and kept his gaze tipped down, concealing his face.

"I heard you were out of the smuggling business," the man said in a light, easy voice. "But I didn't expect to see you in law enforcement."

"I'm not," Jackson said in an equally mild tone, even as he calculated how long it would take him to get his gun free. This man knew about his past and had come all the way to Samoa to find him. That didn't bode well, no matter how non-threatening he appeared. "I work part time as a personal protection specialist."

The man grunted in amusement. "A bodyguard. I wouldn't think there would be much need for that kind of thing in a place like this."

"People find things to be afraid of," Jackson replied, easing back a step, trying to get a look beneath the brim of the man's hat. "Even in paradise."

"I suppose so." The man tucked his chin closer to his chest. "And you've always been good at putting people's fears to rest."

"Who are you?" Jackson asked bluntly. His client could be out any minute and he needed to find out if this man was a threat to his or Hannah's safety before that happened. "What do you want?"

The man laughed. "I'm a ghost. But a friendly one. I don't mean you or your wife any harm. I saw her on her way to work this morning, by the way. She's the kind of person who has a smile for everyone isn't she?"

"I'm not going to discuss my wife with you," Jackson said, trying to keep the anger building inside of him from his voice. "And you still haven't answered my question."

"No, I suppose I haven't." The man sighed. "This seemed easier from half a world away. I didn't think it would still feel so raw, but it does. Even knowing she's not Harley, it was hard to watch her walk down the street."

Jackson reached out, gripping the stranger's arm, but the moment the man lifted his face he wasn't a stranger any longer. Jackson pulled his hand away with a shake of his head, certain he was seeing things.

But then, if Harley could come back from the dead, why not his best friend?

"Clay." Jackson shook his head again, still expecting the man's features to rearrange themselves into someone else's face. "I thought you were dead."

"I am. As far as anyone who used to know me is concerned." Clay's mouth twisted into a hard smile. "I can't tell you who I am now. I shouldn't be here at all, but I owe you things I don't owe anyone else. First and foremost among them, an apology."

"You don't owe me anything."

"I do," Clay insisted. "Because I believed her. I believed that you beat her and frightened her and all the other lies she told. I wanted it to be okay to fall in love with my best friend's girlfriend so I let myself believe."

He turned, staring out at the street, where sweating men on bicycles vied for space with tiny, rust-tinged cars. "And when I woke up in a hospital eight months after the crash, I kept on believing for years after I should have realized the truth. There's no excuse for what I did and I'm not here asking for forgiveness."

Jackson started to insist that he was too happy with the way his life had worked out to regret anything that had brought him to where he was now, but Clay turned to him and said—

"I'm just here to let you know that the boy

is mine and I intend to take care of him."

"Harley's son?" he asked, pushing on when Clay nodded. "How do you know? I had a man working on a DNA test, but Harley and the boy disappeared again before he could get a hair sample."

"I have resources at my disposal not even you can imagine," Clay said, a hint of his old humor in his tone. "I know the boy is mine and I know you've been removed from the CIA's watch list."

Jackson's brows lifted. "Is that so?"

"It is. Though I wouldn't plan on a move back to the States anytime soon. Better to give everyone a cooling off period."

"I have no plans to move," he said, his thoughts racing. "My wife and I enjoy island living."

Was Clay CIA or simply higher up some criminal food chain than Jackson had ever climbed? He didn't know and he wasn't sure he wanted to. He trusted Clay's intelligence and he trusted that his old friend wanted nothing from him but to make amends. That was all he needed to know. Anything else would only put him and Hannah in danger.

But he couldn't resist asking for one small favor, for Hannah's sake.

"You won't hurt her," Jackson said softly. "I know she's a monster, but she's also my wife's sister."

Clay looked surprised, but only for a moment before he regained control of his features. "No, I won't hurt her. I haven't changed that much. But I'm going to make sure my son is taken care of."

"Hannah says Harley loves the boy," Jackson said though he couldn't believe he was putting in a good word for the bitch who had ruined his life.

But then, it wasn't ruined. Not anymore. He was the happiest he'd ever been. Hannah was worth the years of rage and all the injustice. She was worth every second of hell Harley had put him through and more.

"You *must* be happy," Clay said with a sharp laugh. "The Jackson I knew wasn't the kind to forgive or forget."

Jackson shrugged. "I had to make a choice between punishing the woman I hated and pleasing the woman I love. It wasn't a hard call to make."

Clay cast an appraising look his way before nodding slowly. "Well, I'm glad for you. You deserve the sweet life on the beach with a pretty girl."

"You know better than most that we don't get what we deserve," Jackson said, casting a glance over his shoulder at the door to the embassy before turning back to his friend. "But don't shut out the good in the world because of a few terrible people. There are good ones out there, too."

"Angels to make up for the devils?" Clay asked wryly.

"Something like that," Jackson said though he couldn't help thinking that Hannah was much more interesting—and far sexier—than any angel. "I'm just saying I learned the hard way how much revenge can steal from a life. I wouldn't want that for you."

Clay's blue eyes softened and for a moment Jackson saw the kid he'd met in basic, the all-American boy who could make everyone laugh, even at the end of a day spent drilling until their muscles had turned to jelly. But then the shadows moved in behind his friend's eyes again, proving Clay was a long way from making his way out of the darkness.

"Thank you," he said though Jackson could tell his words had fallen on deaf ears. "I appreciate the advice and wish you the best. And please tell your wife thank you for me."

"For what?"

Clay smiled. "For getting you back on the straight and narrow before I had to put you in prison."

CIA then, Jackson thought, wondering why that didn't make him feel better about the road his friend was on.

Clay stepped away, lifting a hand. "Goodbye, Jackson, and good luck."

"Be careful," Jackson said, raising his voice slightly to be heard as Clay continued to walk away. "There's always something left to lose, man."

Clay waved in acknowledgment of Jackson's words, but he didn't turn around. A few minutes later he had disappeared in the crowd of shoppers swarming the outdoor market across the street. Jackson had a feeling he wouldn't see the man again.

Later that night, as he and Hannah sat down to dinner on their lanai overlooking the ocean, he told her the news, downplaying his concerns about what Clay would do to her sister.

But she was no fool.

"Well, if Harley had given me any way to get in touch, I'd warn her trouble was coming but…" Hannah lifted her arms helplessly at her sides before plucking her napkin from the table and laying it in her lap. "I'll just have to send extra good vibes her and Jasper's way and hope for the best. There's nothing else I can do."

"Your good vibes are pretty powerful," Jackson said, admiring the way the setting sun caught the red highlights in her hair. "You're beautiful tonight."

"I am not," she said, smiling even as she rolled her eyes. "I was out in the heat sweating in a coconut field all day. My hair is a wreck."

"Your hair is fine and I like you sweaty."

She hummed knowingly beneath her breath as she speared a tomato from her plate. "I know you do, but don't even think about trying anything until I've showered."

"Is that a hard limit?"

"Jackson," she warned, narrowing her eyes.

"What if I wanted to sniff your sweaty panties while you shower?"

"Cheese biscuits," she retorted, plucking another tomato from her plate and tossing it at him across the table.

Jackson dodged easily, suppressing a laugh.

"No." She pointed a finger at his chest. "I'm not giving you my dirty panties."

"That's all right. I can get them out of the laundry basket later."

"Ew, Jackson," she said, wrinkling her nose. "You don't seriously have a stinky panty fetish do you?"

"Would you still love me if I did?"

"Of course," she said, without a moment's hesitation, making his heart feel a little lighter even though he was only teasing. "But it would take some getting used to. I'm not accustomed to sharing that part of my life with anyone but the washing machine."

He reached across the table, taking her hand and lifting it to his mouth. "I'm kidding." He kissed the tips of her fingers one by one, loving the way she flushed in response. "I have no designs on your panties, just the woman who wears them."

She curled her fingers, giving his palm a squeeze. "Harley's going to be okay, right?"

"I think so," Jackson said, knowing he had no choice but to be honest with her. They didn't do lies or secrets, not even to spare each other pain. "I asked Clay not to hurt her and he said he wouldn't, but I haven't seen the man in years. I don't know whether he's still the kind to tell the truth."

Hannah cocked her head. "You did? Really? You asked him not to hurt her?"

"I knew you would want me to."

She sighed. "You are my favorite husband I've ever had."

"I'm the only husband you've ever had," he said, rising from his chair. "And the only one you're going to have. Come get in the water with me."

"What about dinner?" she asked, but she was already standing beside him, letting him lead her down the steps toward the beach.

"Dinner will keep. The sunset won't and I want to fuck you in the waves with the sun in your hair."

And so he did and it was even better than the last time he'd made love to his wife because every day with Hannah was better than the last, every moment more priceless than the one before.

She was all the proof he needed to believe that life was beautiful, nearly as beautiful as the woman in his arms.

***

Ready for more dark, sexy romance?
Sign up for Lili's newsletter to receive a
free preview of
her next hot, erotic series:

Acknowledgements

First and foremost, thank you to my readers. Every email and post on my Facebook page has meant so much. I can't express how deeply grateful I am for the chance to entertain you.

More big thanks to my Street Team, who I am convinced are the sweetest, funniest, kindest group of people around. You inspire me and keep me going and I'm not sure I'd be one third as productive without you. Big tackle hugs to all.

More thanks to Kara H. for organizational excellence and helping me get the word out. (No one would have heard of the books without you!) Thanks to the Facebook groups who have welcomed me in, to the bloggers who have taken a chance on a newbie, and to everyone who has taken time out of their day to write and post a review.

And of course, many thanks to my husband, who not only loves me well, but also supports me in everything I do. I don't know how I got so lucky, man, but I am hanging on tight to you.

Tell Lili your favorite part!

I love reading your thoughts about the books and your review matters. Reviews help readers find new-to-them authors to enjoy. So if you could take a moment to leave a review letting me know your favorite part of the story—nothing fancy required, even a sentence or two would be wonderful—I would be deeply grateful.

About the Author

Lili Valente has slept under the stars in Greece, eaten dinner at midnight with French men who couldn't be trusted to keep their mouths on their food, and walked alone through Munich's red light district after dark and lived to tell the tale.

These days you can find her writing in a tent beside the sea, drinking coconut water and thinking delightfully dirty thoughts.

Lili loves to hear from her readers. You can reach her via email at lili.valente.romance@gmail.com or like her page on Facebook https://www.facebook.com/AuthorLiliValente?ref=hl

You can also visit her website: http://www.lilivalente.com/

Also By Lili Valente

The complete Under His Command Series
Available Now:

Controlling Her Pleasure (Book One)

Commanding Her Trust (Book Two)

Claiming Her Heart (Book Three)

The Bought By the Billionaire Series
Available Now:

Dark Domination (Book One)

Deep Domination (Book Two)

Desperate Domination (Book Three)

Divine Domination (Book Four)

Printed in Great Britain
by Amazon.co.uk, Ltd.,
Marston Gate.